Runaway Heiress
Billionaire Bachelors
Book Six

Melody Anne

Runaway Heiress
Billionaire Bachelors – Book Six
By Melody Anne

Printed and published in the United States of America.

Published by Exclusive Publishing Company
Salt Lake City, Utah
Look for us online at:
www.exclusivepublishing.com
Email: Info@exclusivepublishing.com

Cover art done by Exclusive Publishing Company

ISBN-13: **978-0615676869**
ISBN-10: **0615676863**

DEDICATION

This book is dedicated to Stephanie. What fun adventures we've had together. I'll never forget Canada and driving across the border with barely any money and no directions. I love you to pieces and we will forever be in the dg club ;p

Books by Melody Anne

*The Billionaire Wins the Game – Book One
*The Billionaire's Dance – Book Two
*The Billionaire Falls – Book Three
*The Billionaire's Marriage Proposal – Book Four
*Blackmailing the Billionaire – Book Five
*Runaway Heiress – Book Six

+The Tycoon's Revenge – Book One
+The Tycoon's Vacation – Book Two
+The Tycoon's Proposal – Book Three

-Midnight Fire – Rise of the Dark Angel – Book One
-Midnight Moon – Rise of the Dark Angel – Book Two

See Melody on Facebook at
facebook.com/authormelodyanne

Melody's Web Site: www.melodyanne.com
Twitter: @authmelodyanne

Coming Soon:
Midnight Storm – Rise of the Dark Angel – Book Three
Final Book in the Anderson Series – Austin's story

Note from the Author

Creating a book takes far more people than just myself. I could never do this without the help of my family, friends and the supportive people I've met along this journey. Thank you to all of you who have read and re-read this manuscript, trying to make sure I haven't left holes in the story, or wrong names. ☺ When reading another author's book, it's easy for me to catch the errors, but in my own material, it's easy to overlook, because I know what I want it to say, so I'll just read it that way. Thank you Nikki for your countless hours of editing and for being so great as to tell me when something really sucks and I need to up my game.

Thank you Patsy, Phoenix, and Lucille for my desperate demands of reading my manuscript and for catching errors. Thank you so much for believing in me.

Finally, thank you to my fans. You are the reason I'll stay up all night to finish something. You are the reason I love my job so much. Your letters and messages of encouragement and pleasure in my stories inspire me to be a better writer. I love Facebook and getting to talk to all of you. I love twitter and all these amazing forms of communication.

Thank you for your reviews, yes, even the negative ones. I've been able to make changes based off of what you want. The bottom line is that without my fans, it doesn't matter if I write. If no one was reading these stories, they'd be nothing more than words on paper. Thank you, truly from the bottom of my heart. I hope you enjoy this newest installment in the Anderson Family. This is a much different story than my usual romance. I was wanting a little bit of an adventure. I hope you enjoy Chad and Bree's story.

Melody Anne

The Anderson Family

Joseph Anderson – married to – Katherine Anderson
Their kids
Lucas, Alex, Mark

Lucas Anderson marries Amy Harper
Their kids
Jasmine, Isaiah,

Alex Anderson marries Jessica Sanders (Jessica's dad John)
Their kids
Jacob, Katie

Mark Anderson marries Emily Jackson
Their kids
Trevor (Mark adopts), Tassia

George Anderson marries Amelia Grant
Their kids
Trenton, Max, Bree, Austin

Trenton Anderson marries Jennifer Stellar
Their kids
Molly (her niece, they adopt)

Max Anderson marries Cassie McKentire

Bree Anderson marries Chad Redington

Austin Anderson marries: to be announced

Prologue

"Rummy," George called as he laid his cards on the table and grinned at his brother. They were both competitive by nature and always trying to one up the other but it never caused hard feelings.

"That's the third game in a row. I think you're cheating somehow," Joseph said while he eyed his brother.

"Don't be a sore loser," George replied, then stood and headed to the bar to pour each of them a drink. "What do you want?"

"I'll just have a Sprite on the rocks. Damn Doc said nothing harder than carbonation for me until my blood pressure comes down," Joseph mumbled. George poured Joseph a Sprite and himself a nice glass of aged whiskey. He received a glare when he sat down, sipping it in front of Joseph.

"Quit glaring, I'm not the one with the medical problems," George said with a laugh. Joseph shrugged his shoulders and sat back. It was late and Katherine would be expecting him soon.

"Make any headway with Bree, yet?" Joseph asked.

"I don't know what's been going on with her lately. She's restless. If only she'd settle down," George trailed off.

"You know Chad's back home." Joseph let his sentence sink in.

"Mmm, definite possibilities there, that boy can't be easily intimidated," George replied as the wheels in his head started turning. Bree could barely look at a man before her brothers scared him away. Now, Chad wasn't only strong, but had been friends with Mark and his brothers since they were kids. He wasn't easily pushed around and George had a feeling he could put up with a lot without breaking.

"Maybe it's time we have a family dinner, a nice welcome home party for Chad," George said, his eyes lighting up. He was afraid Bree was pulling so far away from him he'd never get her back. He'd also received some worrisome letters, lately. Most of the time his security staff assured him hate mail was harmless, but one particular type of letter had come in repeatedly. They feared it was from the same person… and the man wasn't backing down.

"I think you're right. We'll have dinner on Friday," Joseph agreed. The two men made plans long into the night, their spirits rejuvenated with another matchmaking mission on the horizon.

Chapter One

"It's so good to have you back, Chad. Are you home permanently?"

"Yes, It's time for me to retire from the military and settle down," Chad answered Joseph. They were sitting in Joseph's inviting den, catching up. Chad had been out of the country more than in it over the last twenty years. He'd joined the military right out of high school with his missions being top secret, he wasn't often able to talk to his friends for months on end.

"I'm glad to have you home," Mark said. He'd missed his friend. He knew Chad was dealing with a lot of demons, but hopefully being around friends would help.

Chad and Mark had a lot of similar features, both tall with dark hair and blazing blue eyes. When they'd been younger, they had used those similarities when on the prowl for women. Chad was virtually a third brother to Mark.

Chad had originally joined the army right out of high school, but after five years and several successful missions, he was recruited by the Special Operations Group to be a SEAL. He'd only been twenty-three at the time and excited to be called up. After a couple years, he'd become secretive.

Then about ten years ago, he'd closed up completely. They knew he was involved in top secret missions and they knew his life was always on the line, but they couldn't do anything to stop it. All they could do was offer their support when he came home. They were grateful he'd decided to retire.

Mark spent six years in the reserves. He'd thought about making a career out of the military, but he'd changed his mind. He had too much love for the land and his personal freedom. He knew you either gave your all, or nothing. Those men depended on each other to stay alive.

As he watched his friend, he almost wished he would've gone with him. Maybe then Chad wouldn't have so many demons to fight.

Whatever his last mission had been, it hadn't been pleasant. Maybe someday he'd open up about it.

"It's time," Chad replied before taking another sip from his bottle.

"Time for what, Chad?" Mark asked.

"That's what I wanted to tell you. I purchased that ranch, south of your place. Everything closed a month ago but I wanted to wait until I saw you to say anything," Chad answered, his face breaking out in a smile for the first time that evening.

"Seriously? That's great! I was thinking about obtaining that piece of land but they told me someone already had it. They wouldn't say who, though," Mark exclaimed. He'd been upset when he found out the land was purchased without being placed on the market. He'd asked the previous owners to give him first choice, but the cranky old man who owned it said Mark had enough land and didn't need any more. Mark hadn't fought him on the matter but he'd hoped to one day own it and expand his ranch further. He no longer cared, though because he'd much rather have Chad as a neighbor than add acreage he really didn't need.

"You remember Jed? He was friends with one of the kids of the old man. He told me the guy wanted to move to warmer weather so I jumped on it. I need something physical to keep me busy. D.C. offered me a desk job, but there's just no way," Chad said with excitement.

"Hell yeah," Lucas jumped in the conversation. "I'm thinking I'll be out with you guys instead of locked in the office all day."

"I'm not coming out of retirement so don't plan on staying out there too much," Joseph said with a glare directed at his oldest son.

"Wouldn't dream of it," Lucas answered with a chuckle.

"Now that you have the land, when are you going to fill it up with kids?" Joseph asked, making all the men groan.

"There's nothing wrong with marriage and kids. Half of you in this room are already taken, so quit the groaning," George jumped in.

"I'm not as easily lassoed as these guys, so back off," Chad said with a chuckle, though he eyed Joseph for an extra second to make sure he knew Chad didn't want him playing matchmaker. He had a sneaking suspicion the old man had something to do with the marriages of his kids and nephews. George and Joseph were twin brothers and had got the idea into their heads that life wasn't complete without a whole herd of grandchildren climbing all over him.

Chad wasn't one of their kids, but being best friends with Mark made him a prime target. He could practically feel the arrow aimed straight towards his chest.

"I don't know what you're talking about, boy, but a good woman to warm your bed at night isn't the worst thing," Joseph said.

"I have plenty of women to warm my bed. I don't need to put a ring on any of them," Chad answered back. Joseph shook his head and went back to talking to his brother. The boys all laughed, happy with their small victory. Chad could hold his own any day of the week.

While everyone was occupied, Chad stepped out on the balcony, needing a few moments alone. He'd been bluffing Joseph. He certainly wasn't a monk, but he barely had time for himself, let alone finding myriads of women. He just wasn't interested in tying himself down in a relationship. There were too many complications.

He looked out over the large back yard and sighed. It had been a long time since he'd been able to relax and *smell the flowers*. He wasn't sure if retirement was a good or bad thing. At least with his own land, he could work night and day if he desired. He wouldn't have to answer to another person, and more importantly, he wouldn't be responsible for other people's lives.

"Time for dinner," Katherine called. Chad took a calming breath, then stepped through the door. He kissed Katherine on the cheek as he passed by. She was like a mother to him. He didn't know how his life would've turned out if it hadn't been for Joseph and Katherine. They were the kind of parents every kid dreamed of having. He'd bend over backwards for them – all they had to do was ask.

***

She was sick of it. While she loved each one of her brothers, she was tired of their overbearing, overprotective, he-man tactics. She had to get away for a while, take time for herself and prove she wasn't some delicate flower needing twenty-four hour supervision.

Brianne Lynn Anderson, or as everyone called her, Bree, was the youngest of four children. Her siblings were all strong, stubborn, alpha males who treated her like she was still ten years old, even though she was twenty-eight and a college graduate.

She hadn't managed to keep a boyfriend for longer than a few weeks because once they met her brothers they went scampering for the hills. She was so disgusted with the cowards for running that she wasn't even upset when they left. Still, she'd like to actually find out what it was like to be treated like a woman. She was probably the oldest living virgin in the United States. Her brothers would like for her to die an old maid.

She jumped in her car and quickly hit the gas pedal. Her father had summoned her to Joseph's mansion for a welcome home party for some friend of Mark's, but she figured it was the perfect time to escape from her overprotective family. She jumped on the freeway and started driving south - the farther she pulled away, the bigger her smile became. Freedom flashed over and over in her mind. Even though it was overcast and cold she flipped open her sunroof and stuck her hand in the open air. She laughed with pure joy at what she was doing.

Maybe by the time she returned, her family would realize she wasn't a little girl anymore and they could let her live her own life. She loved them – but she could only take so much pampering.

***

Chad sat on the couch holding a glass of deep amber whiskey, smiling as he enjoyed the warmth from both the liquor and the flames in front of him.

The Macallan sixty-year-old Single Malt Whiskey was like butter on his tongue. He laughed at the idea that anyone would spend sixty thousand dollars on a single bottle of alcohol, even one that tasted as good as what he was sipping. Chad was incredibly wealthy by anyone's standards, but sixty thousand...

Over the past twenty years, Chad hadn't had to spend anything of what he made. Every dime he received went right into investments. Luckily, those gambles had paid off well, leaving him with millions. He'd paid cash for his ranch and it hadn't even made a dent in his account. He'd been so frugal his entire life, changing his ways wouldn't be easy. As his commander had said many times, he needed to live a little, whatever the hell that meant.

The Anderson's made him seem like a pauper, though. He figured when the US government needed to be bailed out in a crisis situation, Joseph Anderson was who they called. He may be exaggerating a bit, but still, the family was America's Royalty.

Chad didn't know why he'd been summoned back to Joseph's place. He'd just been there the previous week for dinner and he needed to get his ranch settled. However, when Mark called and asked for a favor, he would always drop everything and be there for him – just like he knew the same was true of Mark. If Chad needed him, he'd be there – and with back-up.

As Chad looked around the room, the Anderson men began entering. Mark had left him sitting on the couch while he hunted down his father. He was being tight lipped and Chad's suspicions rose when he saw Mark's cousins' step into the room. They eyed him warily and he didn't back down. He stared them straight in the eye, wondering why he felt like he was in enemy territory all of a sudden.

He'd brought back a lot of battle wounds from his years of service, not just mentally, but physically, too. He unconsciously rubbed his rib where a bullet had struck. One more inch to the left and he'd have been dead. All that remained was a minor scar but it was something he looked at often to remind himself to be careful who he trusted. That bullet had come from someone who was supposed to be on the same side as him.

"Sorry to keep you waiting so long, Chad," Joseph said as he entered the room followed by Mark. If Chad had been nodding off, Joseph's booming voice would've certainly woken him. The man had a way of making people stand at attention better than Chad's old commander.

"It hasn't been a problem. I've been enjoying your whiskey," Chad responded as he swallowed down the last of the amber liquid.

"You have excellent taste, my boy. George got me that bottle for my last birthday. It's almost out so I'll have to hunt down some more. It's hard to find truly exceptional products these days," Joseph answered, not even blinking at the five-thousand dollars' worth of whiskey Chad had drank without tasting.

"What was the big emergency?" Chad asked. He didn't want to be rude but he had a lot to take care of and didn't want to stand around discussing liquor.

"I like a man who gets straight to the point," Joseph replied, not answering Chad's question. Chad looked again at Mark's cousins and felt like he was being assessed – and they found him wanting.

"Alright, if you don't want to tell me why you wanted me here, then do you want to explain why your nephew, Max, looks like he wants to tear my head off?" Chad said. He smirked at Max, who looked like he was thinking about stepping over and slugging Chad. After a second, Chad raised his brows at him in a bring-it-on gesture, then smiled as he watched Austin grab his brother's arm when it looked like he was about to step forward.

Chad hadn't been around Mark's cousins much; just saw them a few times when he was in town, but not enough to really feel he knew any of them. They'd never before been hostile, though and he couldn't understand why they felt a need to act macho all of a sudden.

"Sorry about my boys, Chad. We have a situation and my brother and I have come up with a solution that the boys aren't too thrilled about. They can't beat down their sister so they want to take their frustrations out on you," George said as he stepped forward.

"What do I have to do with this?" Chad asked, wanting to know what was going on. He was sick of them sidestepping the issue.

"There's no way to say this but to just come out with it, Bree's gone missing," George said. Chad instantly tensed – his full military training coming to the front. This was something he could handle.

"Have you put in a missing person's report, hired an investigator? Have there been any threats made against her?" Chad fired off questions.

"No, no, it's nothing like that. She was feeling a bit overwhelmed by her brothers and cousins. We found where she is. She's not all that great at hiding, and we were able to trace her credit cards. She's staying in a small town in Oregon. I went there to try to find out what was going on and she refused to come home. She said she was being smothered and she's determined to make it on her own. Apparently, she's refusing to come back until everyone backs off," George said a bit sheepishly.

"Then, I don't understand what the problem is," Chad said with confusion. She wasn't really missing after-all. Why were they acting as if it was an emergency?

"Bree's been very sheltered her entire life. She's never known about the danger involved, coming from a family like ours. She's determined to make it on her own, but she's a target, being my only daughter. I've received threatening letters before regarding all my children, but lately there's been several targeted at Bree. I have surveillance on her at the moment, but I need someone I can trust. Mark regards you as the best man he knows," George trailed off.

"You want me to babysit?" Chad asked with horror. They were asking a bit much of him if they wanted him to keep an eye on a spoiled heiress.

"I know it's asking a lot," Joseph piped in and Chad turned to look at the man who had kept him out of the legal system. If it weren't for Joseph stepping in and taking responsibility for him when he'd been an angry teenager, he never would've shaped up. He wouldn't have joined the military and he certainly wouldn't have the same life he did. How could he refuse him anything?

"We hate to ask you to do this but if any of the family goes down there we know she's going to try to slip away again. She wants to have independence, which I can understand, but she needs to be watched over. This last letter that came in, scares the crap out of us," Mark jumped in.

Chad reached for the note Mark was holding. The words sent a shudder down his spine. Some person was infatuated with her and Chad knew how that could turn out. If she refused the man and he had no hope of winning her over, he very well could take her life.

"What makes you think she won't run if I'm in the picture?" he asked.

"We thought about that, too. She won't like having you there but she doesn't deem you a threat against her independence. Since I moved the family back east for so many years, she hasn't been around you. I know she won't like the idea of you babysitting her, but I don't think she'll take off again just because you're there," George offered.

"Crap, you're asking a lot. If anything were to happen to her on my watch, I'd never forgive myself," Chad said as he ran a hand through his hair and started pacing the room. He felt like he was damned if he did and damned if he didn't.

"You won't let anything happen," Mark said with full confidence. Chad looked at his long time best friend and a look passed between them. Mark was right – Chad would take a bullet before he ever let anything happen to a person he was protecting. His hand rubbed his ribs once more, unconsciously. Never again would he lose a person under his watch – he couldn't survive it, not after his sister.

"Give me the details," he commanded, putting himself in full control. He was in ops mode and he wouldn't let the Anderson family down. Joseph and George breathed sighs of relief, while Bree's brothers stiffened their shoulders. They weren't happy with the arrangements.

"This is stupid, Dad. I say we drag her back here and lock her in the flipping basement. If she wants to act like a spoiled brat, then treat her like one," Max growled as he started pacing.

"Your sister is an adult and can go where she wants. Do you want to drive her further away? This is the best thing we can do for her. If you want to be the one to shatter her world and make her afraid to even leave her apartment, then be my guest," George said while he stood to his full six and a half foot height. He may be getting older but he was still an intimidating man. Max backed down, not from fear, but respect.

"Sorry, Dad, I'm just frustrated. We've had some rocky years since losing mom, and I thought it was finally getting put behind us. I'm worried about her," Max apologized.

"We're all worried," George said while placing a hand on Max's shoulders.

"You know, Redington, if you lay a hand on my sister in any way, I'm going to knock your teeth out," Trenton said with a smile of anticipation. Chad outright laughed at him. No wonder she'd ran – they really did act as if she was a teenager, instead of a twenty-eight year old woman.

"Tell you what, Anderson, if she doesn't do it first, we'll have a go," Chad said. Trenton sized him up for a moment, before his shoulders relaxed and he realized what an ass he'd made of himself. Finally he laughed and the rest of the tension fled the room.

"I think we'll get along just fine," Trenton said as he stuck out his hand. Chad felt like he'd passed some kind of test he didn't know he was taking until it was over. He shook the man's hand, then they all sat down and gave Chad the details on where Bree was and what to expect once he got there.

He knew she was going to be a handful but he was suddenly anticipating his babysitting duty. She wasn't hard on the eyes and he was curious about the fire he knew was just below her uptight surface. He may actually find the next few months enjoyable.

As if Trenton could read Chad's thoughts, his eyes narrowed for a moment. The two men stared at each other before Lucas said something and broke the moment.

Chad had always liked a challenge and it seemed two were being placed before him. First he had to somehow tame the princess, and secondly, her brothers didn't want him near her. He fought back the smile wanting to stretch across his face. He didn't need to make the situation any more tense right then.

Chapter Two

Bree felt like someone was watching her. She looked around and didn't see anyone, but she could feel the little hairs on her neck rising. Something wasn't right – it felt like someone was out there – staring a hole into her. It was dark and she was uncomfortable walking to her car alone. Normally, she never thought twice about it. She was in a small town, virtually no crime to speak of, and she knew she had nothing to worry about.

But still…

She picked up her steps, moving faster toward the parking lot. Reaching into her purse, she frantically searched for her keys. She'd feel better once she was locked inside her car. The only reason she was paranoid was the frustrating phone conversation she'd had with her father earlier in the evening.

He'd tried to demand she return home immediately, saying her safety was in jeopardy. She knew it was purely her family overreacting, once again. She was sick of the babying. She was a grown woman and would prove to them she could make it on her own. They'd get a hoot out of the fact she was shaking as she approached her vehicle.

Bree turned her head again and looked around, then laughed inwardly at her own paranoia. No one was there – the boogeyman wasn't after her. She looked down and searched through her over-sized purse – muttering under her breath that first thing in the morning she'd finally purchase a clip so she could attach her keys to the handle. She always took an hour to find the dang things.

After several frustrating minutes, she realized her car keys weren't in her bag. She must've left them on her desk, grabbing her office keys instead. She'd done that too often to keep letting it happen. She sighed and turned to walk back inside. Her employment was mindless work, but it gave her a paycheck and she didn't have to spend from her trust fund. She was determined to live on her own dollar – not her family money.

Though she knew she was being ridiculous, her hand closed around her purse. She knew it wasn't a weapon, but it held enough items that if she hit someone over the head with it, she'd probably stun them long enough to get away. She was irritated at how paranoid she was acting. Her father's call must've spooked her more than she realized.

She slowly made her way back to the office, trying to act as normal as possible. She wished at least a few other people were out so she wasn't totally alone. Though her heart raced, she held her head high and stepped around the back of the building, to the employee entrance. She looked around at the two-story structure, seeming to spot shadows shifting in every corner. She pulled out her phone and pushed a button on the side so the screen lit up. It made her feel better to have a trace of light. She needed to talk to the manager about fixing the exterior lighting. It wasn't safe for employees to be going in and out of the alley at night in pitch black.

Just as she was about to turn the corner a cat screeched, then rushed past her legs, its hair brushing against her bare calves. She must have jumped five feet in the air. The sound could've been bottled and used in a horror flick.

She realized the humor in the situation and immediately started laughing out loud uncontrollably. She had to stop being so paranoid. She finally pulled herself together and turned around the back of the building - and slammed into something solid.

Trying to get her breath back and move at the same time, she realized it wasn't a wall she'd collided against. Arms were tightening around her in a death grip and her vision blurred as all the air left her body. She was momentarily paralyzed with fear. She knew she needed to scream, kick, bite, do anything other than stand there. People were still inside the office building. If she could get their attention she'd stand half a chance.

Bree finally managed to drag in a lungful of air and opened her mouth wide to let out a scream. As if he knew what she was doing, his hand clamped quickly over her mouth, further escalating her panic. She couldn't die in an alleyway behind a crappy office. She pushed against his hand and bit down, pleased when she managed to get her teeth around some of the flesh of his palm.

"Crap! Stop that. I'm not trying to hurt you," the man growled. His voice wasn't reassuring. She also wasn't a stupid teenage girl who believed her assailant only wanted to talk.

She continued twisting her body, but it was like struggling against the bars of a roller coaster car. He wasn't budging an inch. The more she struggled, the stronger his hold became. Managing to lift up her foot, she slammed her three-inch heel down on top of his. He let out a yelp and released his grasp.

She didn't take time to turn, but started running for the street. She only made it a few steps when his hands grasped her arm and she was pulled up tight against him again. This time he lifted her clean off the ground. She continued to struggle, knowing she only needed one good shot at his body. If she could get away a second time, she was ditching the shoes and running for all her life was worth.

"If you calm down I'll let you go," he commanded. Yeah, right. She wasn't buying that either.

She managed to swing her elbow backward and connected with his rock-hard abs. She immediately whimpered as pain shot through her arm. She may as well have slammed her elbow into a brick wall.

"Damn, your dad could've told me you were hell on wheels," he muttered as he took a few steps toward the wall, then flipped her body around so she was facing him. His words took some of the wind from her sails. What did he have to do with her father? She'd heard about kidnappers saying a family member was sick to get you to go with them – that had to be what it was.

As he stepped into the street, the light shined down on them and she got her first look at her attacker. Bree's eyes widened in surprise. She knew the man was built like a truck, since she'd been pressed against him for several minutes now, but his face was stunning.

She forgot to fight him as his glacial blue eyes looked down into her own. Even in the darkness of the night she could see they were unusual in color, almost purple verses blue. Maybe he was wearing colored contacts as a disguise or the dim light was messing with her head. But, he couldn't hide his chiseled features. He looked like he was cut from granite, with his strong jaw, high cheekbones and perfect nose, which was flaring at the moment. He had a small scar running from the corner of his eye to his ear that only added to his appeal. His hair was cut military short, making her wonder if he was some kind of mercenary.

Bree realized she was ogling him, and how ridiculous that was. She pulled herself together and put on her haughtiest expression. Growing up with three older brothers had taught her how to at least project confidence, even if she didn't really feel it.

"I'm not stupid. I've heard all the tricks attackers use. There is no way you're getting me into your car. I don't care if you say you know the freaking Pope. If you let me go right now, I won't press charges," she snapped.

She saw red when his lips twitched as if she was amusing him. He thought she was funny. She was ready to scratch his eyes out - and anyone would stand witness that she wasn't normally prone to violence, but he had her held against her will and then had the nerve to mock her.

"I somehow don't believe you on that count but since I'm not attacking you, I have nothing to worry about."

"If you aren't some crazy stalker, then who are you?" She demanded to know, proud her voice wasn't shaking. She knew she'd break down if she made it out alive, but she was standing strong, at least for the moment. She didn't know if her knees would give out once he released his grip but she hoped the adrenaline kept her upright until she was safe.

"If I release you, will you try to run again or are you going to listen?" He asked with another smirk. She was so ticked off she found herself curious of what he wanted. Who was so arrogant as to try and abduct someone and then have the nerve to want to chat?

Obviously this man.

"I'll hear you out, but as you can see, my phone is in my hand and I activated the emergency button on it. The sheriff is on his way here, now," she bluffed. He looked at her hand, then up to her eyes. She had a feeling he knew she was lying but he didn't call her on it, giving her the illusion of regaining some control in the odd situation.

Chad smiled at Bree. He found he was enjoying himself immensely with Mark's cousin. He knew she was going to be spitting mad when she found out he was sent to babysit her – even madder than she already was, thinking he was a crazy sex stalker.

"Chad Redington," he finally said and she looked at him with a blank look. He said his name as if she should instantly know who he was. Maybe he had escaped from a mental hospital. She took a step back and he immediately narrowed his eyes. She pulled in a ragged breath. She was trying to be careful, not wanting to cause him to strike.

Then her eyes widened as she concentrated on his name. She had heard it before. She searched her memory trying to remember why the name sounded familiar. She looked him over again in his dark jeans, skintight T-shirt and worn cowboy boots. All he needed was a hat, spurs and a horse and he'd be riding off the pages of a *Louis Lamoure* book. Her mind must be playing tricks on her because, though the name sounded familiar, she didn't know him. She decided it was time to leave.

Bree quickly turned as she got ready to bolt, but once again his arms snaked around her and suddenly she was pinned against the wall, his body pressed tightly against hers. She felt every inch of his solid thighs, washboard abs and arms of steel touching her. She forgot how to breathe.

"Listen, I've told you I'm not here to steal your virtue. Your father sent me," he said, his breath sweeping over her face, his lips only inches from her own.

Bree had been afraid and upset before his words, but her head about exploded when he said he was sent by her father. If he was lying, he needed to get more creative. If he was speaking the truth, her family members were dead – every single one of them. She in no way needed, nor wanted, a babysitter.

Chad's eyes lowered their gaze to her mouth. She felt him push a little closer and she knew he'd finally realized they were pressed together against a brick wall in a secluded alley. She was suddenly aware her breasts were tightly pressed against his chest, making her heart rate accelerate. She became even angrier to actually feel anything other than fear and loathing toward the man holding her captive.

He loosened his grip and moved his body back, just out of reach, but his hands stayed planted on the wall on either side of her head – caging her in. His close proximity wasn't helping her brain to function properly.

"Why would my dad send you to stalk me?"

"He didn't. I'm here to protect you. He told me you're aware of the threats against you," Chad said. He was done playing. She was affecting him in ways he hadn't expected, and certainly didn't want. He was there for a job and nothing further.

"I will tell you the same thing I told my father. We've all received threats our entire lives. It goes with the territory of being from a family like mine. I won't validate this pathetic man or woman's addiction by living my life in fear. I don't need, nor want a bodyguard. You can go back to my father and tell him, *No thank you*," she spat, then looked pointedly at his restraining arms. He was about to get bit again and this time she'd sink her teeth in even deeper.

"Your dad told me you'd say that. He also told me to tell you, he was the one in charge, and come hell or high water I wasn't to leave your side, so take it or leave it, but I'm here to stay," he said with a smile.

How could he infuriate her and turn her body on at the same time? She wanted to take a bite out of him, but she wasn't so sure it was to cause pain, anymore.

"I'll just give the local sheriff a call and tell him someone's stalking me," she said with confidence, while smirking at him. She knew her rights. He couldn't stalk her without consequences.

"Go ahead and give Captain Musket a call. We go way back, as a matter of fact, we served on the same team for several years," he answered. Bree's eyes flashed with fury at his words. Men! And they all stuck together.

"Can you please let loose of the arm cage so I can get my keys and go home? I'm tired, cranky and very much done with this conversation."

"After you," he said while taking a step back. She swept past him and went inside to grab her keys. She sat down and called her father. Just because he said her dad had sent him, didn't necessarily mean he was telling the truth.

"Hello," her father's voice came over the line. He was answering his own phone, which meant he knew the call was coming in.

"Did you seriously hire a babysitter for me?" Bree didn't take time to say hello. She knew she didn't need to say who was calling. If her father had indeed hired Chad, he'd know exactly what she was talking about. If he hadn't, he'd have the entire National Guard at her office in less than five minutes.

"So good to hear from you twice in one day," George answered. By him ignoring her question, she had her answer. She was silent as she fought the urge to scream into the mouthpiece of the phone. She knew she couldn't get any more words past her throat so for the first time in her life she hung up on her dad.

He deserved to know how incredibly ticked off she was.

Chad was indeed sent by her father. She knew she could plead, threaten and shout but it wouldn't do her any good. Her father wouldn't pull him from his task. In her father's opinion, if she insisted on being on her own, then she would have to deal with a shadow. After taking several minutes to wash her flushed cheeks, she decided she was ditching her unwanted escort.

She crept to the front of the building and snuck out the main doors. Hopefully she could shake him and drive off before she realized she was gone. She was sure he knew where she lived, but if she could beat him home, get inside and lock the door, she'd come up with a better plan the next day.

There was no way she could handle the very appealing Chad Redington hanging around her, day in and day out, without eventually ripping his shirt off with her teeth, button by button.

Bree reached her car with no sign of Chad, and quickly jumped in and tore out of the parking lot. She was feeling pretty smug and incredibly proud of herself until she noticed the headlights of a car trailing close behind her. There was no way he could've caught up so quickly. Hopefully it was just another motorist but she had a feeling it was him.

When the car followed her down the driveway to her incredibly small rental, she knew she was busted. He most likely would start lecturing the second they emerged from their cars.

She pulled in front of her house and flew from the driver's seat. Her hands were shaking as she jumped up the steps and tried to get the key in the lock. She was planning on slamming the door before he had a chance to follow her.

"Did you really think you could ditch me that easily? I'm trained in hunting people down," Chad said, startling her. She turned from her stubborn doorknob and there he was, leaning against her porch rail as if he didn't have a care in the world. She hadn't even heard his car door slam, nor the normally squeaky steps as he came up behind her. She needed to become a lot more aware if there really was a stalker out there.

"I told you back at the office, no one wants to harm me. No one is out to get me. My father and brothers have always been too over-protective. They're all just mad because I snuck off right underneath their arrogant noses. I have to prove at some point that I'm perfectly able to take care of myself. Go away, you're trespassing," Bree snapped as she finally got her key in the stubborn lock.

"So, those threatening letters meant nothing."

"I've already told you, it comes with the territory. If I went into hiding every time I received a pathetic letter, then I'd never get to leave the house."

"Your father said it's been escalating. If he's concerned enough to hire me, then you have something to worry about." Bree gave up. There was no use arguing.

"Look, I'm not trying to frighten you but your father had surveillance done near the place you work and there's been suspicious activity going on. I don't have all the details but it seems there's been a car parked near your office, with someone taking pictures," he said, hoping to finally get through to her.

"I'm sure it has nothing to do with me," she said, though a chill went down her spine.

"You are ridiculously stubborn. Do you care so little about your own life?" he snapped.

"I'm tired and need a cup of coffee. You can leave now."

"I'm not going anywhere," he replied, folding his arms.

"Well, enjoy your time on my porch then, because you're not invited inside," she snapped as she pushed open the door.

Bree looked up and her heart stopped beating for a moment. Her entire body tensed and she felt dizzy.

Someone had been in her house – and her belongings were strung all over the place. The message on the wall was what had her close to fainting, though.

You're mine.

It was written in what looked like blood.

Chapter Three

Chad saw her tense and he immediately straightened from his relaxed position. He grabbed his gun, lifted her out of his way, and stepped inside her front door. Bree could do nothing but stare as he walked inside. What if the person was still there? She started to follow him.

"Wait here," he commanded. She glared at him, but knew he would hold firm so she crossed her arms and waited as he searched her home – his entire body in stealth mode. She held her breath, sick she couldn't do more than stand there frozen. When her lungs felt like they were about to burst, she finally let the air out and sucked in fresh oxygen.

As Chad stepped through each room, he was on full alert. He was in his element – the hunter, searching for prey. He hated leaving her alone on the front porch, but didn't see an alternative until he cleared the house. He quietly made his way through the small dwelling, checking every square inch. Finally, he relaxed when he was satisfied the house was clear.

As Chad looked around her homey place, he started to think she may not be who he originally thought she was. He knew she had a trust fund in the seven figure range, but her home was quaint. Instead of flashy pieces of art or over-priced furniture, he saw second hand pieces, lovingly restored, and homemade Afghans hanging from the back of the couch. Her father told him she was refusing to touch her trust, but Chad hadn't believed she'd be able to hold out. No way could she go from being a spoiled princess to an everyday working girl. He didn't see it happening… but the evidence was right in front of him.

He made his way back to the porch, uncomfortable with how long she'd been out there alone. The crime scene was fresh, which meant the people who'd done it could be hiding nearby, waiting for a chance to get their hands on her.

"They're not in the house," Chad said as he joined her on the small front porch. "Now, do you understand the need for a bodyguard? They aren't playing around, Bree. What if you'd come home when they were still here? This night could've ended far worse than you can imagine," he said. She said nothing as she stepped across the threshold. Her once cozy cottage style home was destroyed.

The stress of the situation finally set in and Bree's body began trembling as she looked at the words splashed across her entrance hall. Why would anyone be out to terrorize her? She couldn't comprehend it – she hadn't done anything to deserve it. There wasn't a trail of broken hearts in her wake. She couldn't think of a single person who'd want to terrorize or harm her.

Bree felt violated as she looked at her belongings scattered across the floor. They'd destroyed pictures, antique furniture, and treated her possessions as nothing more than garbage. A tear slid down her cheek as she picked up an Afghan her mother had made. It was ripped apart beyond repair.

"Why would someone do this?" She choked, finding it difficult to get the words past her closed throat. Irreplaceable items were gone forever. She rubbed her face against the quilt her mom had spent endless hours creating – it too destroyed. As if ripping it to shreds hadn't been enough for them, they'd even spilled a foul smelling liquid on it. She let it drop from her fingers and flutter to the floor.

"There's no explanation for it. Some people get off on terrorizing others. Whoever did this isn't finished. They want you scared, but they're also warning you. If you look at statistics, you'll see a pattern. A lot of crime could've been prevented if the victims had only paid attention to the warning signs. I think you should go home, but if you insist on staying, I'm not going anywhere," Chad said, taking pity on her and wrapping his arm around her shoulders. She knew she should pull away but she needed comforting and she couldn't bring herself to struggle against him.

"If I run home, they win. I won't give them that victory, along with the satisfaction they received causing this damage," she insisted.

Chad sighed as he pulled her closer. She was stubborn, far more than her brothers, which he didn't think was possible. He would feel a whole lot better if she'd realize the danger she was in and go home – but he knew it wasn't happening, at least not yet. She wasn't scared enough.

"If you're going to insist on hanging around then make yourself useful and help me clean this." Bree stepped away from him and grabbed a garbage sack. Chad didn't say anything further, just quietly stood by her side and helped her clean. Within a couple hours the house was back to normal – all damaged items either tucked out of sight or thrown away.

"I've had a hard day, I'm going to bed," Bree stated and walked from the room. She knew she wouldn't get him to leave and she didn't have the energy to fight any more so she left the evening's frustrations behind her as she walked to her bedroom.

Chad watched Bree make her way down the hallway. She was standing strong but he could see the weight of the world on her shoulders. She was strong, but eventually even the strongest person needed to let someone else carry the burden for a while.

A few minutes after her door shut, he heard her shower running and his body tightened with need. What was wrong with him? She was his assignment – nothing more, nothing less. He shouldn't feel sympathy, anger, and certainly not desire. It was time to get out of the house for a little while. He'd do a perimeter check around the property.

Even with her out of sight, his thoughts refused to turn from her. Bree was stunning, but obviously didn't try highlighting her assets, instead hiding beneath layers of clothes. He knew what was beneath her clothes, though, since she'd been pressed tightly against him. He groaned as his pants grew tighter. He'd never had such trouble distancing himself, but then again, he'd never had such a beautiful assignment.

Hopefully, she'd come to her senses and just go home. Then, he wouldn't have to worry about the consequences of sleeping with his best friend's cousin. Damn, all of her brothers would stand in line to kick his ass if they knew he was so much as thinking about touching Bree.

He grinned, thinking a good fight would do his libido some good. He needed something to get his mind off of her naked, wet and lathered up body standing beneath a stream of hot water.

Pull it together, you're not a horny sixteen year old, Chad berated himself. Then he jogged into the surrounding woods next to her house. She would have to live in the middle of nowhere. Why not make it easier for the crazy person after her!

He completed the search of her property and knew it was time to return to her house. There was no one around and luckily there was only one driveway leading to the house so if a car approached, he'd hear it. On the bad side was the fact that someone could get incredibly close on foot before he was alerted. The tree's came within twenty yards of her back door. He'd have to set up better surveillance.

He promised her family nothing would happen to her and he was going to make sure nothing did happen on his watch. He stepped inside the doors and his stomach knotted. What was she trying to do to him?

Bree turned and gave a tentative smile as Chad walked in. She frowned when she saw the scowl covering his features. She didn't understand what his problem was. She looked behind him and nothing seemed amiss so she shrugged and went back to cooking. She wasn't the one who'd asked for his invasion into her life and she didn't see why he was in a bad mood. If anyone had a right to be grouchy, it was her.

Chad gritted his teeth when he saw Bree cooking, wearing a pair of shorts showing off entirely too much of her long, beautiful legs, and a fitted tank top. Was she trying to see how far she could push him before he snapped? Did she want him to wrap his arms around her and take her against the kitchen wall? He was close to doing just that.

He sat down and adjusted his pants for what felt like the hundredth time and tried to look anywhere but at her. He knew he should walk away – leave the room. Find any other place to be, other than a few feet from her but his eyes kept drifting back to the shapely curve of her thighs. He could easily see she was a runner. Her legs were toned and tan and seemed to stretch for a mile.

She was only about five and a half feet tall, making her head fit perfectly underneath his chin. She was the right height for their bodies to fit like a glove while he lay on top of her, thrusting inside. *Crap!* He admonished himself silently. He absolutely couldn't go down that road. Being in her presence was the same as throwing a lit match into a dry hay field. He was burning up.

Before he realized what he was doing, he was standing behind her. He couldn't seem to stop the forward movement. All his inner lecturing and self-pep-talks weren't penetrating his own thick skull.

"Do you need help?" he asked, taken aback at his own husky tone. He wasn't holding himself together well. He could imagine what his team would think of his behavior. They'd probably be on the floor laughing – no probably about it, they'd definitely be cracking up at his expense.

"No, I got it…" Bree started to say as she turned around. When she realized how close he was, her eyes widened. He watched as she looked from his neck, then tilted her head up, up, up to stare into his eyes. Once she reached their deep azure depths, hers widened even more.

Their gazes remained locked together, and he was losing the battle to maintain distance. Just one kiss – he could allow himself a moment of pleasure. They were both consenting adults – and no one would be hurt by a simple kiss. He was sure it wouldn't be as great as he expected. One kiss, then he could get back to his job of guarding her - minus the sexual tension.

Chad slipped his arm around her back. If she gave even a hint of protest, or resisted in any way, then maybe he'd get a little sense back into his head. But instead she melted like butter against him. She never removed her eyes from his and her body seemed like it was made to fit only him. She sank against him, her eyes seemingly surprised by their behavior. One taste, he promised himself. He'd only have one taste of her, then he'd let go and get their relationship on a strictly professional basis. If he couldn't, he'd tell George he had to find someone else to guard his daughter. He couldn't protect her if he couldn't keep it professional.

His heart pounded as he leaned forward. His body tightened even more, and the sigh escaping her lips sent his heart racing. She was turning him inside out.

"Just one kiss," he muttered out loud without conscious thought. Her eyes slid shut as his mouth edged closer. She was openly inviting him – he was doing nothing wrong.

Before his lips made contact with hers, there was a loud pounding on the door. Chad wanted to rip apart whoever dared to interrupt them. He swore aloud before he was able to stop himself. Bree's eyes slightly opened as she looked at him with confusion. It was obvious she hadn't heard the knock. She was wondering why he hadn't closed that final gap between them.

The pounding on the front door grew louder and Chad pulled back, forcing himself to concentrate. He didn't think her stalker was going to make his job as easy as knocking, but then again, there were criminals that stupid.

He pulled his gun from his belt and silently approached the front door. He didn't see the fear creep into Bree's eyes at the sight of the deadly weapon. He'd carried it for so long, his hand felt empty without it – like something was missing. When he peaked through the curtain, he let out a frustrated breath, causing Bree to nearly panic.

"It's okay," he assured her before stepping to the door and flipping the lock. Did her siblings have built in radar? *My sister's about to get violated by her bodyguard, we'd better hurry over there.* He was grateful for his many years of service; otherwise he didn't think he'd be able to pull himself together so quickly.

As four huge men stepped through her doorway, Bree went from frightened to angry in two-seconds flat. She loved her brothers and cousins, but she had left to get away from the interference, not have them keep following her around. She hoped Chad wouldn't say anything to them about the break-in or they'd really freak out on her.

"Where are Larry, Mo and Curly?" Bree asked with an innocent smile.

"Lucas, Mark and Austin couldn't make it," Trenton stepped up and answered, knowing exactly who she was referring to. "Charlie stepped up to take their place, though," he finished, pointing to his long-time best friend.

"How you doing, kiddo?" Charlie asked as he stepped forward and enveloped her in a bear sized hug. All the air was immediately squeezed from her body as he embraced her overly tight. He'd been doing it since they were kids and it always made her feel awkward.

Charlie had always been the pimply faced band geek, but he'd shot up about eight inches in high school and joined the football team, where he and Trenton had become inseparable. He'd practically lived at their place. Now, he worked for the corporation so he'd transferred with them during the move a few years back. She was glad he was there but could do without all the manhandling.

Charlie noticed Chad putting his gun away and narrowed his eyes at the weapon, but kept silent. No one else seemed to think it was out of place for Chad to be sporting a deadly weapon in Bree's tiny living room.

"Did Dad send you?" Bree asked when Charlie finally released her and she could breathe again. She noticed immediately when Chad stepped too close to her in a bodyguard manor. Who the heck was he protecting her from? Her brothers? She'd like to pound the over-sized, macho men, but she didn't need protection from them. She looked at him quizzically but he didn't take his eyes from the group of men.

She stared back and forth from her brothers, cousin, and Charlie, to Chad, and found it almost funny how they were all standing so rigid, almost in preparation for a brawl. Last she knew, her family had been who'd hired Chad so why did they seem like they wanted to rip him to pieces?

Chad's libido was still revving to go, and from the look on her family member's faces, they knew it – and weren't happy about it. They glanced from him, around her room, then back, seeming to realize they'd jumped their sister from the frying pan into the fire. She needed protection, but it was obvious they were thinking she may need a chastity belt as well – at least in his presence. They were probably right.

"Is there something wrong with visiting?" Max asked as he finally broke the odd standoff and stepped forward. He gave Bree a much gentler hug before stepping back. That seemed to trigger the others to step forward and hug her. When they were finished, she sighed and headed to the kitchen.

"I guess not, as long as that's all you're doing here. I'll make fresh coffee," she offered. The sooner they got to the real reason for the visit, the sooner they'd leave her in peace. She'd prove to them she didn't need to run home. After her house getting vandalized, she needed to prove it to herself as well. She was still extremely shaken from her stressful day.

"Nice to know we're so welcome," Alex said with sarcasm, but the smile he threw her showed he didn't have any hard feelings.

"There's not a whole lot of room but we should all fit around the table," Chad said, taking over and leading them to her hardly adequate dining area. The men looked at the chairs skeptically, but gingerly sat, letting out relieved sighs when the chairs didn't break. Chad remained standing against the counter and Bree turned so he wouldn't see her smile. He was still in alpha-dog mode, protecting her, maybe without even fully realizing what he was doing.

"Getting mighty cozy in this place, aren't you?" Charlie asked, his entire attitude was yelling loud and clear that he didn't like Chad and didn't want him in Bree's home. It seemed Charlie was a little jealous. He decided to poke him a bit.

"We're making do," he said with a lazy smile. His comment earned him glares from all four men. Chad knew he could take them out – or he was cocky enough to think so, but he wouldn't want to do that to Bree – they were her family.

"Okay, enough of this posturing. I don't know what the heck is going on in this room, but the testosterone is flowing in sickening waves. I thought you were the ones who hired Chad in the first place," Bree said, her tone full of irritation. No one spoke for several moments, then Trenton let out a chuckle and soon Max and Alex joined him. Charlie continued to glare.

"Sorry, sis. Dad wanted Chad to babysit… I mean act as a bodyguard," he quickly corrected. "None of us were thrilled to have someone so… well… um…" Trenton trailed off, seeming at a loss for words for the first time in his life. Bree finally put the puzzle pieces together and her grin spread in victory. Oh, the fun she was going to have for all the crap her family put her through.

She walked away from the coffee pot and stood right in front of Chad, who looked at her suspiciously. He knew she was up to something, but he had no idea what. She could see the concern in his eyes. Good, he was messing with her hormones; it was time to mess with his.

Before he could stop her, Bree leaned into him, pressing her body tightly against his and landed her lips on his frowning mouth. Her arms reached up and pulled his head down to hers. He was so stunned, he allowed her control over him for about two-seconds. Then, his body took over.

The electricity between them caused him to forget all about their surroundings and her family being in the room. He forgot everything and focused solely on the way he felt with Bree in his arms. She felt better than a cool lake on a hot summer's day. His arms snaked around her and he immediately deepened the kiss. Just when he was ready to pick her up and cart her to the bedroom, she pulled away on shaky legs.

Bree took a breath, her heart pounding as she tried to control her reaction from the kiss. She hadn't known it would cause her head to spin. She was trying to make a point and instead she felt like she was on a boat in the middle of the perfect storm. She turned to see all four men shooting daggers at both her and Chad. Good – she'd gotten the reaction she wanted. It helped calm her thundering heart.

"So, *what*, Trenton? Young? Masculine?" Bree mocked. She gave them a Cheshire cat smile as she turned back to the counter and pulled down six coffee mugs. She set them on the table as if nothing was wrong, then began pouring hot liquid into each cup.

Trenton was in shock at Bree's behavior but he finally pulled himself together and sent first her and then Chad a smile. It was obvious Chad didn't appreciate being used. He could instantly see Bree was playing them all and he wasn't giving her the victory of knowing she'd done a great job of causing him more stress. He grabbed his cup and took a large gulp, not even wincing when the hot liquid burned his tongue and throat.

"I don't care how you react, Bree. You need someone to protect you and Mark and Uncle Joseph both vouch for Chad so it looks like you're stuck with him. If you want to act that way, have at it," Trenton said, calling her on her bluff. Her shoulders slumped as her plan backfired. She forgot how good her brothers were at one-upmanship.

"Fine, as you can see, we're just comfy cozy here. There's no need for all of you to hang around, too," she said as she sat down.

"Sorry for hassling you, Chad, but we tend to worry about Bree," Max said, further shocking Bree. It seemed they were deciding it was smarter to team up with Chad than to fight against him. She figured they knew if he was their buddy, she would no longer want to side with him. He'd become more of an enemy than a friend. They were right.

"I'd feel the same way if it were my family. Mark is like a brother to me, and Bree being his cousin is a good enough reason for me to want to protect her," Chad answered, all his animosity seeming to evaporate. *Great, just great*, Bree thought, *next they were going to sing 'Save the World' and start a bonfire.*

"Has anything happened since you got here?" Alex asked. Bree tensed, not wanting Chad to talk about the break-in. He ignored her as he looked at the men.

"Someone broke into her house," he answered, which had all four men sitting up straight in their seats again.

"What the hell, Bree! Why didn't you say anything sooner," Trenton shouted. She expected that kind of response from him.

"First of all, I didn't tell you because it just happened today. Secondly, I'm a big girl and can take care of myself. Finally, you guys hired this over-the-top bodyguard for me, so no one has a chance of getting near me, anyway."

"Someone came pretty damn close," Max interrupted.

"I wasn't here," Bree fought back.

"This is getting ridiculous. I should just throw you over my shoulder and drag you home, whether you like it or not," Trenton threatened.

"Over my dead body," Bree shouted.

"You're not going to be acting so tough when some maniac knocks you over the head and drags you away," Charlie said, speaking up for the first time in a while.

"That's not going to happen. You all need to settle down. I've agreed to let Chad stick around, so cool your jets."

"Your stubbornness is going to get you in too much trouble one of these times," Max stated.

"I'm trying to have a normal life. I don't think I'm asking for too much. Give me a chance to live a little, then I'll be the good little girl and come home. I will make sure to get nice and pregnant, run around the house barefoot and serve you all," Bree said with sarcasm, but real pain was in her voice too. She needed them to trust her – to let her live.

Max was the first to cave. He couldn't stand seeing his sister hurting. He got up from the table and pulled her from the chair so he could hug her.

"You know we just love you too much to ever let anything bad happen to you, right?"

"I know," she conceded.

"Since you've agreed to let Chad stick around, we'll back off. But, we would all feel much better if you'd just come home. I promise to even back off if you do."

"I know you'd try, but it would be impossible for you. Just give me a little while to see what it's like to make it on my own. I promise if the situation takes a change for the worse, or if I really do feel threatened, I'll come home. I barely got here, though. I need more time." Bree didn't want to upset her family so she was willing to make some concessions, especially when they were being reasonable instead of threatening or trying to exert their will on her.

"I don't like it, but I'll agree. We all love you, and you know there isn't anything we won't do for you," Trenton spoke up. "We'll take off for now, but remember, we're only a phone call away. You know, barefoot and serving me drinks is good enough. There's no need to get pregnant," he finished in an attempt to make her smile. It worked, as he knew it would. Her brother was one of the good guys, he just had to learn she was grown-up, not the little five year old sister in pigtails, anymore.

"I thought the plan was to drag her back, even if she was kicking and screaming," Charlie protested. Chad shot him a glare.

"Bree's an adult. I think she made a valid point," Chad said.

"We'll let Dad know you're all right," Max said.

"I'll try to keep him from camping on your doorstep," Trenton added.

"Jessica said you can stay at our place anytime. She also told me to tell you that she'd keep all of us ridiculously over-zealous guys away from you. Her words, not mine," Alex stated with a sheepish smile.

"Tell Jessica I'll think about that. Now, get out of here. I love you all," she said, relaxing since she knew she'd won a small victory. She also knew it wouldn't last. They'd go home and immediately begin worrying over the break-in, then they'd be back again, trying to get her home. She should get at least a week or two of peace, though.

Chapter Four

Chad paced the small house from one side to the other but felt like punching out a window instead. He only made it about six steps before he reached one end and had to turn around again.

Bree's family had left a couple hours ago and she was still hiding in her room, where she'd rushed as soon as the front door had closed.

He didn't want to pressure her but he knew she needed to talk. They hadn't had a chance to discuss the kiss that had almost gotten out of hand. They also needed to discuss the living situation. He didn't like the poor security of her house and felt he could do a much better job of protecting her in a more secure location. She was too easily ambushed where she lived but convincing her to leave wasn't going to be an easy task.

He approached her door and listened, feeling like a peeping-tom. Finally, he knocked but there wasn't an answer. He started to worry so he opened the door and peeked his head in, knowing she'd be furious with him, but willing to take the risk. Seeing her sitting on the bed with her head in her hands, looking defeated wasn't what he wanted. The creaking of the door hinges quickly brought her head up and she composed her face, but it was too late, he'd seen the grief, and he wanted to make it right.

"I told you I need to be alone for a while," she snapped.

He took a relaxing breath before stepping inside her tiny space. He tried to avoid the fact that they were alone in her small room. She looked so enticing sitting on top of her purple bedspread.

She tried to keep her glare centered on him but he could see the fear behind her bravado. She was frustrated and didn't want to run home, but her family had brought more worry to the forefront of her mind. He sat down to comfort her. She flinched when he reached his hand out.

"I don't need anyone else coddling me."

"I know you don't but you've been given a lot to handle the last couple of weeks and even the strongest of us can use a friend to vent to sometimes," he calmly replied.

"I know my family wants to keep me safe and I know you have a job to do but I'm sick of feeling smothered. They treat me like a child, instead of an adult. I came here to gain independence, but it seems I'm not even allowed that," she pouted. Chad had to carefully compose his features to make sure a smile didn't come through. She'd probably haul off and hit him if she saw even the hint of a grin.

She said she was an adult and didn't want to be treated as a juvenile, but at the moment she was throwing a bit of a tantrum. The situation was amusing and helped ease the anger inside him that had been building since he saw her tossed house.

"I'm going to share something with you that I don't talk about to anyone – ever," he quietly whispered. "I had a sister – she was the cutest little girl in the universe. I was ten years older than her and I worshipped the ground she walked on." The tone of his voice instantly put Bree on alert. She didn't think his story would have a happy ending, especially when he used the word, *had*.

"My mother wasn't a great person, not even the tiniest bit, and my sister wasn't planned. My mom was so messed up she didn't even realize she was pregnant until she was five months along. She tried to abort her, but it was too late at that point and the doctors refused to do it. Mother was working at a little diner when all this came to pass and the manager was a real decent guy. Apparently, he'd had a crush on my mom for a long time so he jumped at the opportunity to date her. She was down and out and searching for a sugar daddy, and he was the only guy offering, so she accepted. We moved in with him and his place was heaven compared to the trashy apartment we'd been living in," Chad spoke in a monotone voice. Bree grabbed his hand without either of them realizing it.

"My mother was a user – she took all she could from Ray. He was real nice to me. She stopped doing drugs long enough to get through the rest of her pregnancy, but she only did that because she liked living at Ray's place. She didn't have to worry about the bills, or food. She had my sister and wanted to give her away, but she knew the gravy train would end if she did, so she brought her home." Chad paused and Bree was shocked to see moisture in the corner of his eye. He turned away and took a moment to compose himself before continuing.

"Mother had nothing to do with Jackie from the day they came home from the hospital. Ray and I named her. We were the ones who fed and changed her. She was amazing. I don't know how something so perfect could come out of someone so horrible, but she was an angel. She hardly ever cried and she had this smile that would light up the room. The first time she laughed, I couldn't help but join her. It seemed like only days, but all of a sudden three years had gone by. My mother was gone more and more and I could see how upset it made Ray. He offered to marry her but she always managed to delay it. We both knew she was out with other men – sometimes she'd be gone for a few days, then walk in as if nothing was wrong. Jackie didn't even call her mom."

Bree was horrified as she listened to Chad speak of his past. She certainly got upset with her family but she knew how much they loved her, and she loved them without question. They had grown distant after their mother passed, but she'd never doubted their love. They had all just needed time to heal from the tragic loss of losing their mom.

"I was watching Jackie – which was nothing new. I loved spending time with her. I know that sounds weird, because at that point I was thirteen, and most kids that age would feel put out by having to watch a baby sibling, but I loved her so it was never a burden. Besides, I knew she needed me." His voice grew more hoarse the longer he spoke. Bree knew she couldn't interrupt him, though she wanted to stop what was coming.

"We were at the park watching a few kids playing touch football. I took my eyes off her for just a moment, not even half a minute. She was playing on the large fort and laughing, having a great time. I looked at the game, for the first time feeling a little envious that I couldn't play with them. I heard someone scream and jerked my head back to where I'd last spotted her. She was grasping the rail at the top. I jumped up, but before I even reached my feet, she slipped and fell to the ground. It was like the entire event happened in slow motion. One minute she was laughing, the next she was falling. It wasn't even that far, but she was so tiny, and she landed wrong. Her neck broke – she died instantly."

The pain in his voice ripped Bree apart. He was fighting to keep it inside, but even decades later, the wound was only a scratch away, just underneath his skin that she had thought was so thick. She couldn't even comprehend going through what he had.

Tears streamed down her cheeks as she listened to him talk about his sister's last moments. What an imaginable thing for him to witness. Why was he telling her about it? What could she do to make the pain end?

"Apparently there was a pole that came loose. She leaned on it, and fell through. She grabbed another bar, but before anyone could help, she slipped. If I'd been next to her, she'd still be alive today. My mom showed up at her funeral, even managed to force a few tears. She ate up the sympathy from strangers. There was a huge article in the paper and crowds of people flooded the service. I hated them, every single one of them. What right did they have to be there! I was supposed to watch her. The guilt tore me in two. My mom got a huge settlement from the city and took off in the middle of the night. She never looked back and I've never tried to seek her out. After she left, Ray couldn't handle me. I was angry and holding onto so much guilt that I was striking out at him – on everyone."

Bree scooted closer and wrapped her arm around Chad's trembling form. He was in another place at that moment, but he seemed to draw comfort from what she was doing so she stayed pressed against him.

"Ray finally dropped me off at a human services office and I went into foster care. I was tossed from home to home. Nobody wanted to deal with a messed up kid like me. Finally, I ended up in the juvenile courts. That's where I met Mark and Joseph. They saved my life. I was on a path to destroy myself, but they wouldn't let me. They were doing volunteer work and took me under their wing. Mark and I became best friends, and Joseph helped me realize Jackie's death wasn't my fault. I still, to this day, feel responsible, but I know I didn't cause her death. I just never ever want to lose someone again who I'm supposed to watch. Your family feels the same way,

Bree. They love you, and if something were to happen to you, it would destroy them," he finished.

His words made Bree feel about two inches tall. She was so blessed, with a family who loved her enough to go out of their way for her, and she was being stubborn. She still needed to prove her independence but she'd accept having her own personal bodyguard without complaining about it.

"I'm sorry," she finally said, feeling the words were inadequate. She knew they couldn't take away the pain, but she felt helpless to do anything more. What did you say to someone when they opened up to you the way he had?

"It was a long time ago. I just wanted you to understand how much your family loves you – and also understand why I can't let anything happen to you. They'd never forgive themselves if those threats against you were real and they did nothing to stop the man. I can't sit back and not give this my all – I've committed to guarding you, and isn't it better to be over-protective than not protective enough. It's all done for the right reasons."

Both of them were silent for a few minutes and Chad finally realized that Bree was practically wrapped around him. The heat of her body was more effective in healing his wounded soul than any amount of therapy he'd gone to, insisted upon by Joseph.

As he closed his eyes and felt the tender touch of her hand caressing his arm, and the press of her rounded breast pushing against his chest, he felt the sorrow always present, ease and instead his body came to life.

He suddenly needed her with a vengeance. He knew she could take away the pain. The touch of her small hands, the feel of her silky skin, the sway of her body. Without thinking it through, he leaned down and his mouth connected with hers.

The kiss wasn't gentle. It was filled with despair and need. He was trying to push away his demons and quench his thirst. Bree paused for only a moment before she was kissing him back with her own hungry need.

Chad's body instantly hardened. He pulled her onto his lap and his hands explored her back, moving along the slender slope of her spine. She moaned into his kiss, igniting fire inside him. He moved his hands below the hem of her shirt and broke the kiss only long enough to pull her shirt off. Then, before either of them could come to their senses, his mouth connected with hers again.

His tongue pushed against the barrier of her lips and slid inside the warm recesses of her mouth. He greedily took all he could from her, but she wasn't a victim. She clawed at his head, tugging him closer to her, groaning into his mouth. He unclasped her bra and tossed it aside, needing to feel her untethered breasts pressed against him.

He pulled back to shed his own shirt, then pulled her body tightly against his. The feel of her bare breasts pushing against his chest intensified the ache in his groin. Her nipples were hard as they pressed against his skin – sending a shudder straight through him.

He laid her back on the bed and took a moment to gaze down at her beautiful body. She was stunning, her skin flushed with arousal, her breasts rising and falling with the deep breaths she took. Her blue eyes were shining with excitement. Moving his head down her neck, he tasted a slight hint of coconut on her skin.

"Chad," she cried out when he circled his tongue around the top of her full breasts. He cupped their perfect weight in his hands and ran his thumbs across her tight pink buds. Her back arched off the bed, begging him to take her in his mouth. He gently nipped the skin around the peaks, but didn't give her what she so desperately wanted.

She pushed her hips up, grinding her pelvis against his straining erection. He groaned as the movement caused sweat to break out across his overheated body. Finally, he took one of her peaks into his mouth and she cried out in pleasure as he gently sucked her deep within his mouth, then moved back and gently raked his teeth across the sensitive nipple.

She gripped his head in her hands, pulling him closer. He moved from one peak to the other, giving them equal attention, while his hands moved down her body and undid her pants. When he moved his mouth down the gentle slope of her stomach, nipping the skin, then gently soothing the pink bites with his tongue, she arched into him.

She tasted like heaven.

He reached her lower stomach and inhaled her sweet scent, loving the feel of her quivering body. She was soft and smooth and had the most succulent curves. Her hips fit perfectly in his large hands. It took all his power not to strip her and sink deep inside her heated folds. He couldn't ever remember wanting a woman so badly it made him ache.

He slowly pulled down her shorts, sliding them past her feet and onto the floor. With his masterful tongue trailing along the inside of her thighs, she continued to groan beneath him, her legs opening in invitation. He looked up at the red satin covering her from his view and his pulsing manhood jumped inside his pants, causing him to cry out. He stood and removed the denim and his boxers in one swift movement.

He nearly lost it again at the sight of lust in her eyes as she took in his naked body. There was no hiding her reaction from him – desire was evident in her eyes and trembling form. He dropped back to the bed and ran his tongue up her thighs, pausing at the juncture of her thighs.

"Please, Chad," she pled, reaching her hands down, trying to pull him to her.

He ripped her panties off, then leaned forward and swiped his tongue along her silken folds. The first taste of her made his head spin. He nearly came before he ever got the chance to sink inside her.

Chad inserted two fingers into her soft lips and groaned when he felt how ready she was for him. He took her pulsing skin into his mouth and flicked his tongue around the swollen nub while moving his fingers in and out of her. Her body began shuddering, then she tensed and cried out as she gripped him tightly. He swiped his tongue across her a couple more times, wanting to draw out her pleasure.

"Please, too much," she cried, and he finally lifted his head. Damn, she was beautiful, with her half closed eyes, flushed skin and satisfied smile. He had to join them together.

He quickly crawled up her body and brought his mouth back to hers. She tried to turn her head, exhausted from their lovemaking, but he knew he could bring her more pleasure.

He gripped both her hands with his and held them above her head while he trailed his lips across her own, then down her throat to her breasts, where he lavished attention on her swollen nipples. Her hips began to gently grind against him and then intensify, signaling she was ready for him to take her.

He moved his body above hers, his swollen head pressed against her opening. Her eyes widened as he started pushing inside. She was so wet and tight, he had to pause half-way inside, or risk their love-making ending before she could be satisfied.

"More," she demanded, which brought a small smile to his face. Then she moved her hips and all humor fled.

Chad thrust deep inside her in one quick motion and her body stiffened as the full length of him stretched her. Afraid he was hurting her, he tried to pull back, but as her body adjusted, she relaxed and clamped her legs around his back. She pushed her hips up, not wanting to release him and he couldn't hold back any longer.

Chad let go of her hands and moved his arms down so he could grip her hips. He held her soft flesh as he started moving in and out of her tight body. She groaned as the pressure began building again, and he felt her grip him even more. His entire body was covered with sweat, making them slide together beautifully.

He pushed his upper body up, pressing their hips tighter together so she could move her lips down the column of his throat, swirling her tongue around his pounding pulse, then further, until she took his nipple into her mouth and gently bit down.

He completely lost it and quickly thrust in and out of her. She eagerly met him, pushing up, their hips colliding. He felt her stiffen in his arms seconds before she let out a cry of pleasure, then she started pulsing around him. He thrust inside her – in and out, then collapsed as he spilled his seed deep inside her wet folds.

Neither of them spoke as they gained control of their breathing again. He was burning up inside and out, and trying to find the energy to move, when she slowly moved her hips beneath him. He was still buried deep inside and he felt himself stir at her movement. His eyes opened in amazement. He couldn't understand how he could possibly feel any passion after the earth shattering orgasm he'd just had.

"Mercy – I'm begging you," he pled as he finally pulled from her sheath and turned them so they were on their sides facing each other. Her face turned scarlet as she looked at him.

"I… I… wasn't…" she tried to say.

"Thank you," he said as he gently kissed her. He felt utter exhaustion overtake him as he lay next to her. She tensed for a moment, but he wasn't letting her retreat. They could fight when the morning came.

Right then, he felt better than he ever had before and he just wanted to hold her.

He wouldn't let the guilt wash through him, or think of the job he was supposed to be doing. He would fall asleep with her in his arms, and when morning came, they could deal with the world. He reached out and flipped off her light, then pulled her against his body, and fell asleep with a smile still on his face.

Chapter Five

Chad woke up with Bree pressed tightly against him. He took a few moments to gaze at her face – so innocent in sleep. She looked young and carefree in the early morning hours. With reluctance, he untangled himself from her arms and legs, almost changing his mind when she grumbled in her sleep.

He sat on the edge of the bed while she twisted around, reaching out her arm. She finally found the pillow and pulled it against her chest, then sighed as her deep breathing resumed.

Chad quickly used the shower and dressed, then peeked in the door at her still sleeping form. He smiled, hoping she didn't wake before he was finished with his surprise. She'd been through a lot in the last twenty-four hours and she deserved to wake up to something positive.

He searched her fridge, grateful to find all he would need, and then he got to work. Within a half hour he was ready and found a makeshift tray that he loaded and carried to her room. She started to stir when he sat down on her mattress. The smell of fresh coffee must have woken her.

"Mmm," she groaned as her eyes slowly opened and she looked around.

"Good morning," Chad said as he leaned down and kissed her soft lips. She tensed as her eyes opened fully.

"What… What time is it?" she stuttered, unsure of how to act the morning after.

"You have plenty of time to get to work, it's only six-thirty," he answered.

She looked from his face to the tray on her night stand. He'd made her his specialty dish, the one and only thing he knew how to cook to perfection, a Denver Omelet with crispy bacon, hash browns and toast on the side.

"Sit up and I'll hand you the tray. I thought after the day you had yesterday, breakfast in bed would be just what the doctor ordered."

Bree slowly rose and Chad placed the tray on her lap. She looked down as she fought to keep her tears from falling. No man had ever done something so sweet for her and she was having a difficult time maintaining her composure.

"Thank you," she finally murmured as she picked up the coffee and took a sip. It was perfect.

She lifted the fork and took a bite of the omelet and once again her eyes widened as the fluffy masterpiece practically melted in her mouth.

"This is delicious," she exclaimed before shoving another bite in. Before she knew it, her plate was clean and she gave him a sheepish smile.

"I never get to eat so well. I'm usually running late and lucky to have time for a piece of toast. That's one thing I miss from home. Dad has the best cook in the world," Bree said. She polished off the rest of her coffee, then knew she had to get up and ready for her busy day.

"I'm glad you liked it," Chad said, feeling pleased with himself.

"Thank you," Bree said. "I don't want to be rude, but I have to get ready for work…" she hedged. She didn't want to climb from her bed naked, and she was currently sitting there, wrapped in nothing but a thin cotton sheet.

"Before you get ready, I have a gift for you," Chad said with a smile.

Bree looked at him to the small box in his hand. Her eyes rounded in excitement mingled with fear.

"Don't worry, it's nothing too extreme," he said as he set the box in front of her.

She reached out tentatively as if the small package would somehow strike her if she moved too quickly. Chad gave her an encouraging smile.

She untied the bow and opened the box.

"Oh, Chad, it's beautiful," she gasped as she pulled out the necklace. It was a small locket on a thin gold chain. "Help me put it on," she demanded as she exposed the slender column of her throat.

With almost trembling hands, Chad held the dainty chain and clasped it around her neck. The slight feel of her satin skin sent awareness zipping through him. He had to leave now.

"I'll take these," Chad said as his eyes drifted to the swells of her breasts, where the sheet had slipped. She tightened it back up while he grabbed the tray and exited the room.

Bree leaned her head against the wall and groaned. Oh, the man should come with a warning label. He was drop-dead-gorgeous, made love like a god, and could cook, too. She'd never survive if he hung around her night and day. Right then she decided to take it a day at a time.

***

The days started drifting, one into the other and before Bree realized it, an entire month passed. She and Chad had found an easy rhythm, comfortable in each other's presence, but he didn't try to take her to bed again. She almost wished he would. She couldn't make the first move, but she also wouldn't resist if he did.

They watched movies together, laughed, yelled and had some pretty intense standoffs. He was still too over-the-top most of the time, but she also got to see a side of him she was sure he didn't show too many people.

He held doors open for her and pulled out chairs. He insisted on paying when they went to eat, though she would point out it wasn't a date, he'd mutter about stubborn women and hand over his credit card.

The thing that scared Bree the most was how dependent she was becoming on him. She was asked out by her co-workers often on Friday nights, but she refused. She knew Chad would trail along, staying in the background, but she found she didn't want to go out with anyone other than him.

What had happened to her desire to be alone?

She continued to go to work, he followed. She left work and he was right there. No more threats came in – everything seemed to be back to normal so she didn't see any reason for him to stay, though she wanted him to. The thought of making him leave tugged at her gut. She had to firm her resolve and tell him his services were no longer required, because he was creating havoc with her body, which didn't want to listen to her mind. What she really wanted to do was rip every last piece of his clothing away and climb on top of him.

The last few days she'd managed to stop talking to him all together, which seemed to make her die a bit inside.

"Don't you think the cold shoulder is getting a little old?" Bree nearly jumped out of her skin when Chad startled her from her self pep-talk.

"I think it's time for you to admit I don't need a bodyguard. No more letters have come in. No prowlers are lurking around corners. I've called my father and told him, and even he seems to think he may have overreacted."

"That's not what he said to me. He doesn't feel you're safe on your own. If you go back home, you can be rid of me," he said with a mocking smile.

"You're the most frustrating man I've ever met," she said as she jumped to her feet and got in his face. It wasn't an easy task to accomplish, considering he stood a good eight inches taller than her, but with her heels on, she made up some of the difference. Being short wasn't an advantage when dealing with a six-foot-four, muscle bound Neanderthal.

"That's a bit of the pot calling the kettle black, don't you think?" Chad said with a smile.

She pushed her finger into his chest, her temper escalating, along with her desire. She was furious at her traitorous body for wanting the insufferable man.

Chad snaked his hand out and grabbed her wrist, pulling her off balance and causing her chest to fall against his. When she felt the intensity of their touch, she instantly grew moist – her body readying in anticipation of him.

When Bree made a sound low in her throat, Chad's entire body came to life. He'd been killing himself trying to fight his attraction to her. She was the devil in disguise and he knew she'd be the end of him. Simply watching her do the most mundane of tasks, such as bending over to pick something up, sent his body into overdrive. One night of lovemaking hadn't been enough and he was furious at his lack of self-control.

It seemed all rational reactions were out the window where Bree Anderson was concerned.

He pushed his fingers through her silken strands of hair and pressed his lips against hers before he could stop himself. He had to taste her – just for one minute. A moment of weakness wouldn't kill them.

He had to stop.

His job was to protect her – not seduce her in the middle of a public park. They were out in the open with dozens of people walking by. He couldn't seem to get the message to his brain, though. His lips caressed hers until her mouth opened and he felt the tip of her tongue lick against his bottom lip.

His groin jumped to life and he pressed her back against the park wall, his hands tugging on her hair, holding her mouth firmly in place beneath his own as his tongue swept along her lips.

His mind said to stop – but his body needed more.

Deepening the kiss, he forgot everything around them until he heard laughter from some kids, then the sound of kissing noises. He finally managed to pull his head clear and turned to see a group of children laughing at the two of them while kissing their hands.

Bree looked at him through passion filled eyes, leaning toward him, when she finally heard the kids. Her eyes rounded as she turned her head, then her cheeks flushed as she realized the display they'd put on.

She pushed against his chest and he could tell she was mortified by what they'd been doing. Chad kept trying to tell his highly aroused body it just a kiss, not worth getting all worked up over.

"No more," she said breathlessly as she moved away another foot, putting space between them. He wanted to follow and drag her back but he knew she was smart to move away.

"I know. I tend to lose my mind around you," he admitted. She looked surprised by his honesty.

"We can't work together anymore. Obviously I don't use the best judgment around you, and contrary to what you may believe, I don't normally sleep with men I barely know. I'm going for a walk. So help me, if you follow, I'll call the sheriff and tell him you're attacking me," she threatened.

He had a feeling she wasn't bluffing. He decided to give her a little space. Not too much, he still wasn't assured of her safety, but since nothing had happened in a month, she was safe to take a short stroll.

Bree turned and walked down the wooded path. When she reached the bend, he started following. He'd just make sure to stay out of her sight. What she didn't know wouldn't hurt her, after-all.

After five minutes of walking, he figured she was about thirty yards ahead of him. That's when he heard her scream and all bets were off – he shouldn't have allowed her to walk away. He reached for his gun and took off, sprinting down the trail. He turned the corner to find Bree sprawled on the ground.

"What happened?" he demanded while surveying the area. He didn't see anyone, but that didn't mean there wasn't danger.

"A guy tried to grab me. He had a hold of my arm, but I dropped to the ground. He had a knife. He lifted it when I screamed. He was getting ready to grab me again when he heard you running and took off that way," she gasped as she pointed to a small trail.

Chad didn't want to leave her alone, but he had to try to catch the guy. If this was her stalker, he could get him behind bars, where he belonged.

"Go back to the park, now!" he demanded, then took off down the trail. He hoped for once she would actually listen to him. He didn't want her on the secluded trail. He needed her surrounded by the other people at the park – feeling she was safer among a crowd.

As Chad quickly followed the trail, he heard the sound of twigs breaking ahead of him, and figured the guy had about a hundred yard lead on him. It should be no problem to catch him. Picking up his pace, his weapon still drawn, he listened for any changes in the guy's pattern. If twigs stopped breaking, or there was a sudden silence, he could adjust his own stride, but the perpetrator wasn't even trying to hide his departure.

Chad began to hear the sounds of cars and people and realized they'd made a large loop and were going to break out of the trail in a minute. If this guy got into a large crowd, Chad could too easily lose him. He picked up his pace, but when he heard the snapping of twigs stop, he knew it was too late.

He pushed himself even faster and quickly ran into the grassy field surrounding the park. People were milling about, but he didn't see anyone running. He surveyed the area, seeking anyone who was out of place. He swiped his hand across his forehead, frustration making him want to yell.

He turned toward the swings, where he saw Bree walking to her car. Good, she was fine. He moved in the direction of the parking lot. The guy had to be there somewhere. He had to holster his gun so he didn't have someone calling the cops. He could easily explain himself, but by the time he got out an explanation, the perpetrator would be long gone.

Just when he was about to give up and head back to Bree, he saw a black car pull quickly out of a space. The windows had dark tints, but the driver's side was slightly down, allowing the top of a man's head to be visible.

He knew it was his guy. Racing to the car at full speed, he saw the man's head turn as the car tires squealed, peeling out of the parking lot, nearly hitting a family, who jumped out of the way at the last second. Chad came close to the car when a note fluttered out the window, then the driver peeled out and was gone. There was no way he could catch him.

Chad glared at the vehicle without a license plate, making it impossible for him to turn the plate numbers in to the police. He jogged over and grabbed the note the man had thrown out. He was afraid to read what was written on it.

Fury coursed through him as he lifted the note. What the hell did the guy want with Bree? The freak had touched her, nearly managed to abduct her. Chad was acting like a love-sick boyfriend instead of her bodyguard.

A bad feeling began stirring in Chad's stomach. The danger was seemingly gone, but he'd learned from his many years of service to never ignore his gut instincts. He headed quickly toward Bree, feeling an urgency in his movements.

Chad was halfway across the parking lot when a shot rang through the air. Several people screamed, as bodies dropped to the ground – parent's quickly throwing their bodies over their children.

Chad reached Bree and threw himself in front of her, while dragging her behind a large car. Once he made sure she was safely down, he poked his head out and looked for any sign of the shooter. He couldn't see anyone. They must have a sniper, which meant they weren't safe anywhere. He needed to get her to safety.

Chad could feel Bree trembling beside him – maybe she finally realized the amount of danger she was in. It wasn't the time to lecture – he had to get her to safety first. There was an eerie silence through the park. Every few seconds he could hear the choked sob of some of the terrified people, who'd only been out for a nice time with their families. He had to move – they were too vulnerable where they were.

"I'm going to lead you through the cars. We're bait where we are. You need to follow directly behind me, and when I say move, don't hesitate," Chad whispered with authority in his tone. Bree nodded, her eyes huge in her pale face.

"They don't care who they hurt, do they," Bree practically sobbed. She was far more terrified for all the innocent children around the play area than she was for herself. She didn't want to die, but if a child got shot because of her, she'd never be able to forgive herself.

"No, they don't. They want us, not the kids. We just need to get you out of here right now."

"Not us – me," she replied.

"Look, I've been in far worse situations in other countries. This is a piece of cake, comparatively. I'm not going to let anything happen to you. Just do what I say and we'll get out of here," he said with confidence. His commanding voice had a way of soothing her. She put her complete trust in him and nodded her head.

As they began to move, they made it three cars forward without further shots fired. Bree could see her car about five spaces down. She didn't know how they would get in and get away without getting shot, but they had to have a goal in mind, and right then, that goal was her car. If they could somehow reach it, then everything would be okay.

"There's too big of a gap between the last car and yours. Give me the key. I'm going to make a dash for it. I'll get in and pull up to you. As soon as I pull up I want you to get in the back door and lay down on the floorboard. We're going to haul ass out of here. No looking back," he told her. Her gut clenched with fear. She didn't want them to separate – not even for a few seconds.

Chad dashed away before she could argue any further. She knelt shakily next to the small red car, but stayed focused. She watched as he neared her car – keys ready. A relieved breath escaped as he opened the door and started to climb in.

Then another shot rang out and she watched in horror as his body jerked and he was slammed into the side of her car. She watched, paralyzed with fear, as a crimson stain spread across the back of his shirt.

Where was he hit? Was it fatal? He dropped to the ground and a guttural growl crept from her throat. Who were these people? Why were they targeting her – and why did Chad have to take a bullet meant for her?

She watched a man in black step from between a van and truck about fifty yards away. He was heading straight for Chad - she knew he planned on finishing what he'd started. He wanted to make sure Chad was dead. She couldn't allow that to happen. If he wasn't fatally wounded already, she certainly wouldn't hide while he was murdered right before her eyes.

Bree jumped up, exposing herself to the people after her. She looked around with frantic eyes, then locked gazes with the man stealthily approaching Chad.

"I'm right here, you coward," she yelled. He smiled in satisfaction and his direction changed. Refusing to stand there and make it easy for him, she knew she had to lead him away from all the innocent people – away from Chad.

She turned and started sprinting toward the road. She moved in a zigzag pattern, like she'd been taught to do if someone was chasing after her with a weapon. She ran faster than she'd ever thought she could.

She heard the thundering footsteps behind her and knew he was gaining speed. She thought she heard Chad cry out for her, but she knew it had to be her imagination. She wanted him to be alive so badly, she was starting to imagine his voice. It was in those terrifying moments of fight or flight that she realized how much she was falling for Chad.

He'd managed to seep into her life without her permission. He was protective and loyal, stubborn and charming, strong, yet gentle. *Please be okay*, she silently cried.

Bree heard the squealing tires only seconds before a hand clamped around her waist. Maybe it was Chad, maybe he hadn't gotten hurt. She knew better, but she had to hold onto hope.

There was a creaking sound as a sliding door was thrown open, then she felt her body flying upward as she was roughly shoved inside the moving vehicle. Through terror filled eyes, she looked at the three men, all wearing black masks and smiling in triumph.

She opened her mouth to scream, when a filthy hand was slammed across her lips. She automatically gagged from the vile taste of the disgusting fingers on her. She had to fight to not throw-up. She began shaking uncontrollably as she realized the hopeless situation she was in.

Chad was probably dead. She was being kidnapped to be taken, who knows where, and she may never get to see her family again. What a fool she'd been thinking she was invincible. She should've listened to her father.

Bree refused to give the men the satisfaction of seeing her cry. She glared at each one of them as the vehicle quickly sped down the road. Each mile they traveled, she knew the chances of rescue became increasingly more difficult.

One of the men gripped her hair and yanked her head back, a leering smile on his face.

"I'd love to have a little taste of you," he said, his eyes filled with lust. She shuddered, realizing there were worse things than death.

"Pete, knock it off. You know the orders," another guy growled. Pete looked at her with frustration. She had a feeling if it were just the two of them, she'd be in a much worse situation than she already was.

Pete leaned closer and inhaled the scent of her hair. She pulled her head back as much as she could, with his hand still gripping her hair, and spit in his face. She'd rather he punched her than lay his lips anywhere near her. His eyes widened in rage and she thought she may have just run out of time.

"Enough," another man shouted. She felt another hand press over her mouth, but this one was holding a cloth. Suddenly the world started turning black and her last thought, before passing out, was how she hoped Chad made it out alive.

Chapter Six

Chad struggled to his feet. His shoulder was on fire, but it looked like the shot had gone right through. He quickly cleared his mind and refocused, knowing he had to get to Bree. His wound was forgotten as he did a search of the parking lot.

He turned in time to see a couple of burly men haul her into a large black van and tear down the street. He jumped into her car and threw the keys in the ignition, only to come up with nothing. He cranked the key, and again nothing.

Chad slammed his fist into the dashboard, causing a huge crack, and a curse to fall from his lips. The bastards had dismantled the engine. How could he have been so stupid? They'd walked right into a trap. He was trained to avoid these kind of situations. The lack of any activity over the past month had made him grow lax in his job – that and the fact he was falling for Bree.

He would find a way to get her back. He'd done this a million times over on missions. He briefly thought about hot-wiring the car next to him, but the kidnappers were long gone. He was better off calling for help.

Chad grabbed a sweater from her back seat and compressed his wound. He didn't have time to pass out and he would if he lost too much blood. Next, he made a phone call to George Anderson. He wasn't looking forward to the other man answering.

George picked up on the second ring, and was dead silent as Chad filled him in on the situation. He didn't have time for long explanations – he had to locate Bree and ensure her safe return.

"I need a ride now. I have a plan," Chad said with authority in his tone.

"You'll have a ride in twenty minutes," George said before disconnecting the line. Chad laid his head against the back of the seat and waited for his ride, frustration radiating from him.

"Sir, sir, are you okay?" A woman questioned as she slowly approached.

Chad turned his head and looked at her fear filled eyes. He didn't have time to reassure the people who were starting to get shakily to their feet. He saw cell phones out and figured the police would be arriving shortly.

The idiots couldn't open fire in a public place and not expect the police to respond. Chad sat up a little straighter, wondering where the law was. Why hadn't they already arrived? A chill ran down his spine as he thought about the possibility that maybe Bree's attacks went much deeper than just a single person stalking her. What if they had police help, or other people of power? He was going to get answers and he quickly narrowed his list of those he could trust.

When, not if, but when he got Bree back, he wasn't letting her out of his sight until he knew exactly who was after her, and they were behind bars. She was vulnerable and he didn't know how far the ring of outlaws extended.

"I'm fine, check on the other people," Chad responded, dismissing the woman as harmless.

"But… you… you were shot," she stuttered as if he didn't know a bullet had passed through him. In actuality, he'd almost forgotten about the wound. He'd been hurt much worse in far more dangerous places, with many scars to prove it.

"I'm fine," he snapped. He didn't like being cold but he wanted her gone. He had a rescue to think about and didn't feel like making small talk.

Her face blanched at his tone and she quickly ran away. Several heads turned his way, but no one else approached, taking the hint that he didn't need, nor want help.

Twenty minutes later he wasn't surprised to hear the sound of chopper blades as the Anderson Helicopter landed in a patch of grass a couple dozen yards from him. Mark jumped out and rushed to him.

"We've got a doctor on standby at my Dad's place. Let's get you fixed up so we can figure out where they've taken Bree and then bring her home," Mark said, not taking any time for a reunion. Chad appreciated it – he didn't need to make small talk.

By the time the chopper landed fifteen minutes later on the lawn behind the Anderson mansion, Chad was filled with unbelievable rage. The longer he thought about those idiots placing their hands on Bree, the more he felt the need to smash something.

The two men stepped inside the mansion and Chad rolled his eyes as he looked around the room. Her entire family was there, wearing varying expression, ranging from worry to anger to guilt. He knew how they felt. He was beating himself up inside – she never should've been captured.

"Sit down, Chad. We need to look at that arm," Joseph said as he led him to a chair with a medical table set up next to it. An older gentleman immediately cut his shirt off and started poking at his arm, sending white hot fire down to the tips of his toes. The wound hadn't bothered him until the damn man poured his so called medicine over it. Chad tuned the doctor out, ignored the pain and instead focused on George, who looked about ten year's older right then.

Questions started flying and Chad waited a moment before he told them the story. Every set of eyes was focused on him as he pushed the words past his tight lips. He needed a computer, but it was simpler to explain the situation, than demand access to the internet. It would save time.

"Take these," the doctor commanded, handing him a couple pills and a glass of water.

"I don't need them," he said while looking the man in the eye. After grumbling about ridiculous men, the doctor put the pills away and left them.

"I need a computer. I gave Bree a gift about a month ago, a necklace. I know she's been wearing it daily. Inside the locket is a tracking device. I'll have her location locked down in less than two minutes, then I'm going after her," Chad announced. Everyone froze, looking at him with varying degrees of shock and respect.

A laptop computer was placed before him and just like he said, he had her location within a couple of minutes. She wasn't moving, so it looked like the men were already at their destination. Chad frowned as he pulled up a satellite image of the abandoned looking building. It wasn't going to be easy to sneak up on them, and he feared if they knew he was coming, they would harm her. That wasn't acceptable.

"I'm going with you," Trenton insisted.

"You're not trained, you'll only slow me down. We can't waste time, not with Bree in the hands of these men," Chad replied, knowing there was going to be an argument. The two men stared at each other to see who would back down first.

Finally, Trenton held his hands up and turned to his father. It was either that or the two men were going to end up in a fist fight.

"You talk some sense into him because there's no way I'm not helping with this. We're wasting time here. I can't even begin to think about what these deranged bastards are doing to her."

"Chad, you know her brothers aren't going to stand idly by, so why don't you just tell them what they need to do, give them a crash course in rescue, whatever it is you need from them, because I agree with Trenton. The more of you there are, the greater chance you have of a safe rescue," George said. He was speaking in a reasonable tone but there was an undercurrent of authority in his voice as well.

"She's our sister, we're going," Austin insisted.

"Okay, but you don't make a move unless I specifically okay it," Chad announced.

"To hell with that," Trenton shouted.

"It's either that or you can wait here for us to return," Chad said as he moved so he was standing toe to toe with Trenton. He wasn't budging an inch and he certainly wasn't jeopardizing Bree's safety. What Chad really wanted to do was knock Trenton's lights out, but he knew it wasn't the right time to get into a boxing match – no matter how much better it would make him feel.

"Fine," Trenton conceded.

"We should call the cops," Amy said as she entered the room. The men turned in her direction. She was pale and her eyes were swollen from the tears she'd shed. "I've been trying to convince all of you of that for an hour."

"We told you, baby, we can't do that. If the cops rush in, Bree could get hurt. Plus, as Chad explained, we don't know how far this thing stretches. If these people have cops in their pockets and we notify the authorities, we could be warning them of our arrival. They may figure out Bree has a tracking device on her, remove it, and make it impossible for us to locate her again," Lucas said as he wrapped his arms around his wife. She shook in his arms as her tears started flowing again. She and Bree had become very close over the years and she was terrified for her friend.

"The cars are ready, sir," a man said quietly as he stepped into the room. He took a step back as seven huge men turned to stare at him. "The keys are in them," he finished, then made a hasty retreat.

"Thank you, Armon," Joseph replied, stress evident in his eyes.

Joseph laid his hand on Chad's unhurt shoulder and the gesture instantly calmed him. The man seemed to have magic inside, because he'd been able to do the same thing for Chad as he grew up. He could be spitting mad, or feel completely defeated, and the smallest touch from Joseph would somehow ground him.

"Go get your girl back," Joseph said in a knowing tone. Everyone in the room heard his words and turned to glare at Chad. He ignored them and walked to the front doors. Joseph was right. He didn't know how or when it had happened, but he did think of Bree as his. He prayed he found her safe and sound so he could figure out where it was all leading.

***

Bree woke up and the darkness surrounding her nearly sent her over the edge, into panic. She attempted to move, then panicked even more when she realized her arms were tied to something. She struggled for several long minutes, the ropes securing her arms, tearing into her flesh. Finally, the pain was overwhelming and she lay back silently.

Calm down, you have to keep calm, she told herself. She slowly turned her head and looked around the small, dim room. She was tied to an old army cot and no matter how hard she tugged, she knew there was no chance of breaking either the rope or the metal bed. She had to figure out another way to get free.

Taking several deep breaths, Bree strained her ears to see if she could hear anything. Were her attackers nearby? She couldn't hear a sound. She listened a while longer before giving up. That had to be a good sign. No one was coming after her for at least a few minutes. That gave her time to break free.

She strained her memory to figure out the last thing she remembered. She could recall being in the van with several huge men, then the world going black. They must have chloroformed her. That would explain her raging headache.

She focused on her surroundings. She was in a small room with the windows boarded up. It looked like a house, maybe an abandoned one. She didn't know her location. Even if she managed to break free, she could be in the middle of a huge farm, for all she knew. She tried not to let hopelessness wash through her. She was an Anderson, and they didn't give up. Her father would lecture her for years if she were to throw in the towel.

Her wrist throbbed horribly, but the ropes weren't overly tight. She had nothing but time so she started working on the knots, grateful she could move her hands between the ropes. After what seemed like hours, she was ready to start crying. They weren't budging. She heard footsteps and froze.

There was a sound like someone inserting a key into a lock, then her door started opening. She made her body lay motionless and shut her eyes.

"How much crap was on that cloth?" someone snapped.

"I don't know. I just doused it," another man spoke.

"If she doesn't wake up, we're dead. Make sure she's breathing," the first voice said. She heard footsteps, then a large hand wrapped around her neck, lying against her chest. She forced herself not to panic and to take deep, even breaths, but it was difficult as the man's hands lingered too long. When he finally pulled away, his hand slipped across her breasts, making her skin crawl.

"She's still alive," the guy snarled, as if he could care less one way or the other.

"Why don't we try to wake her? I can think of a few ways that could be fun for all of us." Bree shuddered inwardly and hoped the fear of their boss was great enough for them to leave her be. There was no way she could fight them off in the position she was in.

She fought against shuddering as another hand stroked her body. It took all her strength not to tense as his hands moved over her still form.

"Tempting, but I don't feel like getting shot," the man creepily whispered.

"How would he know?" the other guy whined.

"She'd tell him, dumb ass," the man snapped.

"Who's to say she won't make something up anyway? We may as well get some pleasure if he's going to think we did it."

The other guy hesitated and she could tell he was starting to cave to his friend's wishes. She swallowed back the tears pressing against her throat. She had a feeling her life was about to take a horrible turn for the worse. She pictured her family, Chad, and a hot summer day. She could survive this – she was strong, she tried to convince herself, but when the man's hand landed on her thigh, she knew she couldn't. How could anyone?

"Pete, Dave, get down here," another voice yelled from what sounded like the bottom of a staircase. She must be on a top floor. That was at least somewhat helpful if she managed to get the ropes untied.

"What makes him the boss?" one of the men growled and the hand tightened on her thigh and moved upward for a second. She thought they were going to ignore the order. She was getting ready to kick her legs out. She knew they'd win, but she would fight for all she was worth.

"Now!" the voice yelled even louder. The hand finally left her leg and she heard the welcome sound of the two men retreating from her room. The door shut and she lay silently as she listened to them move down the stairs. She realized they hadn't re-locked her door. It was a sliver of hope in her seemingly hopeless world. If she could somehow get the ropes off, then maybe she could get out of the house.

She worked on the ropes, her mind drifting. She hoped Chad had been rescued. She'd never forget the sight of his blood staining his shirt crimson. She prayed she'd get to see him with her own eyes again. She didn't care about anything else; she just wanted the chance to lie in the safety of his arms one more time. She wouldn't even put her ever-present guard up.

She pictured his hands moving through her hair, his gentle lips caressing her own. It was the only thing that got her though the endless hours as she worked and worked at the ropes binding her. She knew blood was dripping down her arms but she didn't care. At least the pain let her know she was still alive – it gave her hope.

Finally, she started to feel a little give in the rope on her right hand. She'd done something to it and the pressure on that wrist started to lighten. She laughed aloud at the pure joy she felt at her small victory. She started moving her fingers around the loose piece of rope and after more struggling, she felt the rope release and she pulled her hand free. She turned her body, to better see the other rope and began working away at the knot.

She made much faster time being able to see what she was doing. She released her second wrist and then sat up in the bed. It was just the beginning of her flight to freedom, but it was a huge victory. She looked at her swollen wrists in the pale light seeping in through the bottom of the door, and cringed. They were cut up pretty bad but she couldn't feel pain at that moment with the amount of adrenaline pumping steadily through her body.

She got to her feet and quickly fell back down to the bed when her head started spinning. She'd gotten up too fast. She winced as the bed made a loud squeak, straining her ears to see if the men had noticed. She sat motionless for about five minutes before she allowed herself to breathe normally again.

It didn't seem as if they'd heard her. *Okay, I'm out of here*, she thought to herself with determination as she moved away from the bed. She stopped just before she opened the door because she heard shouting and the sound of a gun firing.

***

"There's significant activity in the house and the windows are boarded up. I can't pinpoint her exact location but I know she's in there," Chad said to the group of men who were hiding in the brush in front of the seemingly abandoned house. There were no other homes around for miles and they couldn't spot any security measure in place. The men were either arrogant or just stupid. Chad was counting on the latter.

"I contacted my friend who's a cop I know I can trust. Now that we're in place, we may need his team for back-up. They should be here in about fifteen minutes so we need to move fast. You three take the back, Lucas and I will go in the front," Trenton said.

"I'll wait for one minute. While you have them at a standoff, I'll find Bree," Chad said, agreeing with Trenton's plan.

"It's now or never, boys," Trenton called, then the men went into stealth mode and quickly ran toward the house. Chad counted to twenty while he watched them approach the steps. Trenton stood back, brought his leg up and smashed in the rickety front door.

Immediately, gunfire erupted as shots rang out.

Screw waiting a full minute, Chad thought as he rushed in. He had to get to Bree, and fast. There was no way he wanted her anywhere near the line of fire.

"Get the damn girl," he heard someone shout, then saw a man dart for the stairs. Over his dead body! Chad charged the guy and caught him by surprise. He slammed the butt of his gun into the man's temple, making him crumble to the floor. Then he charged up the stairs three at a time.

"Bree," he called. Being discreet was no longer an option, as the house was an eruption of chaos. He had to evacuate her from the premises as quickly as possible and then notify the guys to stand down. She was their only goal. Let the cops deal with the mess of the kidnappers.

"Chad," he heard Bree's voice filled with hope. A door creaked open, and there she was. She was pale, shaking and he didn't even want to think about what was going on with her wrists, but she was alive.

Chad swung her into his arms, slammed his lips against hers for a fleeting moment, then pushed her behind him and started descending the stairs, far more cautiously than how he'd come up. She didn't say a word, just followed him, her body brushing against his with each step.

They reached the bottom of the stairs and Chad smelled smoke. The house was so old it wouldn't take much for it to become an inferno if a fire had already started. He needed to get her out. He looked around the corner and didn't see anyone so he pulled her tightly against his side and rushed through the room, and straight out the front door, flames starting to creep up the walls behind him.

He looked quickly from side to side and didn't see anyone so he pulled her to the safety of the bushes.

Once they were hidden from view he spoke into the microphone on his shirt.

"She's safe and out of the house – pull out," Chad spoke. There were several acknowledgments, more firing, then he saw the guys racing from the burning house, covering each other's backs.

Chad kept Bree behind him as he lifted his gun and fired into the house, covering the men as they ran from the flames. No one was going to die on his watch. Once the men were safely away he finally focused on Bree.

He ran his hands along her body, checking for injuries. When he reached her wrists, she let out a small gasp. He looked at her damaged skin in the light of day and had to fight the rage wanting to boil over. He wanted nothing more than to go back in that house and destroy the men who'd been foolish enough to harm her.

Instead, he gently lifted her hand to his mouth and softly brushed his lips against her swollen and bloody flesh. He wanted to take her pain away – he should've been able to prevent it.

"I'm okay, Chad. Thank you," Bree told him in a tear choked voice. He pulled her back into his arms and held her tightly, while waiting for her family to join them. He heard the sound of sirens in the distance. Their back-up had arrived.

"I'm sorry, Bree. I promised I wouldn't let anything happen. They never should've been able to get close to you, let alone take you away."

"I was the one acting foolish. You're the one who rescued me. I was so terrified when I saw you fall to the ground. I'm sorry I got you shot," she whispered.

She was barely able to talk, she felt so guilty over him being put in such danger.

"Did they…. they didn't… we should get you to the hospital," he choked. He couldn't bring himself to ask her how bad her torture had been. She seemed to realize what he was trying to say.

"My wrists are the worst of my injuries. They knocked me out in the van and when I woke up I was tied to the bed. It took me a long time to get out of the ropes. I struggled a lot – cutting up my skin in the process. They didn't touch me other than that," she reassured him.

He didn't need to know how close the men had come to doing exactly what he feared. She couldn't even think about it without panic setting in.

"We need to have you checked, anyway," he said, but she heard the relief in his voice.

"I wouldn't know what to do if a man in my life wasn't trying to take control," she said with a small attempt at humor. He gave her a half grin before standing up. He saw the ambulance coming around the corner and he wanted to get her inside it.

"Chad, watch out," he heard Trenton yell. Everything slowed down as he turned toward Trenton, who was throwing his arms in the air. First he pointed to his gun, indicating he was out of bullets, then pointed to his left. Chad turned and realized one of the gunmen had gotten away from them. He had a gun pointed directly at Bree and him.

Chad reached forward to push Bree back to the ground, but she saw the gunman at the same time as he did. She dodged his hand, putting her in danger.

Chad whipped his gun back out and put a bullet through the man's head, but it was too late. He watched in horror as Bree moaned just before her eyes rolled back in her head and blood ran down the side of her face.

She started falling to the ground, but Chad grabbed her before she hit the solid surface. Trenton ran toward them, tears running down his cheeks as he saw the lifeless look on his sister's face. She'd been shot in the head.

Chapter Seven

Chad cringed at the sight of Bree hooked up to so many machines. Wires ran from her arms to the consistently beating monitors next to her hospital bed. She looked so fragile lying in the stark room.

He'd never felt more fear than in those moments when she'd crumbled in his arms, blood escaping from the side of her head. The bullet had thankfully only grazed her temple. Still, so much blood loss – too much. One more inch and she'd be dead instead of in a coma. She'd been in it for two months, now, and the doctors didn't know when she was going to wake up. He'd practically lived by her side, guilt consuming him.

Bree's pursuer hadn't been caught. The men, who'd been holding her captive, said they'd never met the man they were working for in person. Everything was done through the phone. Whoever it was, scared them badly enough, they'd rather sit in jail than give anything up on him, which made Chad think there were some upper level men involved.

Bree's family was wealthy beyond what most people could imagine. With great wealth came even greater power. There were people out there who coveted what the Anderson's had. They weren't afraid of using terror, force, or even murder to get what they wanted. Chad didn't know who was behind the pursuit of Bree, but he would find out – and they would pay.

Chad had argued with the doctors countless times already, insisting they weren't doing all they could for her. She should've woken by now. How could her body be working, yet her mind refuse to allow her to wake? He couldn't understand it.

Bree's family was at the hospital as much as Chad. Her brothers took every opportunity to shoot him dirty looks – though they knew he'd done his best to save her. They, like him, needed someone to blame – so he was the easiest target.

"Mr. Anderson, we have some test results we need to speak about," the doctor said as he walked in the room.

"Go ahead," George replied. He looked like hell, with dark circles taking permanent residence under his eyes, and the loss of about twenty pounds. He was making himself sick with worry. It was hard on him being back in the hospital again. It reopened the wounds of grief over the loss of his wife, and caused a whole new mourning period for him and the rest of the family. Even his voice sounded almost dead – defeated, something Chad had never expected from the powerful man he'd come to know.

"We should speak in private," the doctor said.

"Anything you have to say about my daughter, anyone in this room can hear," George replied wearily. The doctor nodded his head before he gave them the shock of their lives.

"Bree is two months pregnant."

The room went utterly silent as all the men slowly turned their gazes from the doctor to Chad's stunned face. It was obvious those weren't the words they were expecting to hear.

"You're sure?" George finally gasped. The doctor nodded.

Suddenly George's face broke out in a small grin, the first one he'd given since Bree had been abducted and then shot. Everyone was taken by surprise at his reaction.

"Well, I'll be…" he trailed off. He took Bree's hand in his own and looked at his daughter fondly. "I know you can hear us, Bree. You're going to be a momma, so you need to fight real hard and wake up," he whispered in a tear choked voice.

Chad realized he wasn't breathing and took in a huge gasp of air. He was going to be a father. Words failed to describe the extreme myriad of feelings coursing through him.

Fear.

Excitement.

Love.

Each emotion had an equal hold on his teetering emotions. He was going to be a dad. He looked at Bree's still flat stomach and had to fight the itch in his throat.

"Outside, Redington," Trenton snapped.

Chad stood instantly. He could use a good fight. It looked like it was show time. He followed Trenton into the hall, and the rest of the room cleared out behind them. No one wanted to miss the showdown.

Chad smirked at Trenton, trying to push his buttons. He needed to hit someone, but he wasn't going to throw the first punch and have Bree all over him when she woke up – and she would wake.

Trenton took a menacing step forward and Chad felt his adrenaline kick in. It had been a while, but he'd been on many combat missions, and fighting was second nature to him.

"I don't think so, boys," Jennifer called out as she stepped between the two men. "Last time I checked, you were both adults," she snapped.

"This piece of crap violated my sister," Trenton snapped. His wife glared his way and he instantly backed down. It almost made Chad smile.

"Your sister isn't a child, Trenton and this isn't the eighteenth century. If they made love, it was a mutual decision, plus none of your business," Jennifer continued.

"But…" Trenton tried to speak, but Jennifer interrupted again.

"There is no, *but*. They have to work this out on their own, and like it or not, it looks like your sister made her choice and this is the father of your niece or nephew. Do you really want to start a relationship with a fistfight?"

It looked to everyone like that's exactly what Trenton wanted to do.

"As much as I'd like to deck you right now, Redington, my wife has a point. What the hell happened? You were supposed to be guarding her, not seducing her."

"That's none of your business," Chad snapped, frustrated that he wasn't going to get the fight he so desperately wanted. Trenton growled something, then started pacing the halls.

"I need air," he snapped, heading for the doors.

"I'm not thrilled about this but Jennifer's right. Bree is a big girl and can make her own decisions. I'm warning you, though, if you leave my sister high and dry, there won't be a woman around to protect you," Austin said.

"I'd let you kick my ass if I did that to her," Chad said, meaning it. He was ready to take her to the courthouse right then. She carried his child; he would take care of her.

The men stared at each other for several moments and Austin must have seemed happy with what he saw because he surprised everyone when he clapped Chad on the back as he walked by. It seemed he had at least one of the brother's approval.

It didn't take long for the news to spread through the family. After the shock wore off, everyone went into planning mode. Hopefully she woke up soon because they now had two irreplaceable people lying helpless in the bed.

***

Bree cracked her eyes open and felt instant terror. She was choking. She couldn't breathe, and her head was pounding. Where was she? Why were wires tugging on her arms? She forced her eyelids further open and glanced around the small room that had a beeping monitor next to her head.

Her heart accelerated and the machine started making a high pitched sound. Her only thought was that she was in danger and had to get away. She didn't know how she'd gotten into the room.

"It's okay, Ms. Anderson. You're okay," a woman said as she stepped up next to her. Who was Ms. Anderson? Was that her? She didn't know who she was. Panic flared even more as she started thrashing around in the bed, the wires connected to her felt like chains.

"You have to calm down. We're going to give you something to help. We aren't trying to hurt you," the woman spoke in a calm manner. Bree didn't believe her. Danger! There was danger. She didn't know why or how, she only knew she was unsafe.

"Call the doctor now, and notify her family," the same woman said to someone else, and the person quickly left the room.

The woman poked a needle into one of the wires hanging from her arm, while a man held her hands down so she couldn't unplug herself. She felt an instant calmness wash over her. She was still fearful, but the panic was ebbing.

"Where am I? Who are you?" she croaked, the words hurting her throat. She winced. The door opened again and a man walked in. He quickly glanced her way and their eyes locked together. She felt like she should know him, but she didn't.

"Bree?" he asked questioningly, like he didn't know if it was her. She looked at him blankly. Was he talking to her?

"Bree, you're awake," he practically shouted as he stepped forward. She flinched when he reached down and brushed the hair from her face.

"It looks like she may have amnesia. We've called for the doctor," the woman said when Chad looked at her.

"Hi Bree, I'm Dr. Bailey. I know you're a little scared right now, but I'm going to see if I can help you, okay?" the man said. Bree nodded her head, reassured by the tone of his voice. He slowly approached the bed and started checking her vitals while continuing to ask her questions.

After about twenty minutes, the door opened again and more strangers stepped inside. Bree turned toward the doctor, not knowing what she should do or say. The room was too crowded – too many strangers.

"Everything will be okay, Bree. This is your family. I'm going to step outside and speak to them for a few minutes, okay?" The doctor said. Bree had no choice but to nod. She watched as they all left the room. The same woman, who'd originally come in, stayed with her, reassuring her. She didn't want to be alone.

***

"It looks like your daughter is suffering from amnesia, which isn't unusual in a coma patient. I'm going to run more tests, but the good news is she's awake," Dr. Bailey said once they were in the hallway.

George and Chad were both speechless for a few moments. The doctor let them have some time to work through their thoughts.

"How long?" Chad finally asked. It seemed the only words he could get past his throat.

"There's no way to know for sure. She could regain her memory at any time, or it could take months. She may even lose some memory all together. There was no permanent damage to the brain from the bullet wound, but I'm unable to give any definitive answers," Dr. Bailey said apologetically.

"Can we take her home?" George asked.

"I need to run more tests. What you need to remember is that you can't force her memory to return. She needs to come to it on her own. If you push too much on her at once, it can make her retreat further. I know you've had a trying time over the last couple months, but she needs to heal. I'll have more answers for you once I've run those tests," he said before turning and walking away.

"What do we do?" Chad asked, feeling helpless.

"As much as I don't like it, we wait," George answered. Neither man was the type to wait for anything, or anyone, so they both took a few moments to compose themselves before walking back into her room.

Upon their return, Bree's eyes were shut and Chad felt like he was going to throw up. He shouldn't have been gone so long.

"It's okay, she's only sleeping. I know it seems like that's all she's been doing, but this is different.

She will wake up again, but she's only going to be awake for short periods," the nurse reassured them.

George sat by her side for a while before leaving to make phone calls. Chad refused to leave. He wanted to be there when she woke again. The doctor came in a few hours later, but didn't have positive news. There wasn't a physical reason for the amnesia, and all they could do was wait it out and pray she regained her memory.

Chad fell asleep with his head resting on her bed and her hand held securely in his.

***

Bree woke again in the dimly lit room but she didn't feel as panicked as the first time. She looked down and noticed the same man who'd walked in earlier, was sleeping close to her, with her hand gripped in his.

She took a few moments to study his face, which seemed softer in sleep. He had short hair and was built like a tank, but for some reason he didn't scare her. She felt safe with him, which confused her, considering she didn't know who he was. He had to be a good guy, though, if the hospital allowed him in her room.

She lifted her free hand and brushed her fingers against his cheek, which had a few days growth of hair on it. The movement must have startled him because his eyes shot open, fully alert, and they were caught, staring into each other's eyes, both of them holding their breaths.

"How are you feeling?"

"I don't know," she answered. Her head wasn't hurting so much, but she was confused, disoriented and scared.

"I'm sorry," he said.

"Why?"

"You shouldn't be here."

"Where should I be?"

He didn't know how to answer her question. She should be safe, and anywhere other than a hospital. She should be free to do what she wanted, not having to hide – not needing a bodyguard. He didn't know what he should say.

"Home. Safe," he finally said. She looked at him quizzically.

"They said my name is Bree. Who are you?"

"Chad, your boyfriend," he answered, knowing the lie might come to bite him in the butt, but not caring. She carried his child and he didn't know when she'd get her memory back, so it would be much easier if she assumed they were a couple. He felt a twinge of guilt for lying to her, but he pushed it back. He had to protect her and his unborn baby.

Her eyes widened at his words and he could see she was digging in her memory, but not coming up with anything.

"I don't think I like hospitals," she finally said, making him smile for the first time in months.

"I don't think you do, either. I'm not too fond of them these days, myself, but this one has kept you safe," he answered with a chuckle. His laugh made her smile and the slight flush that came to her face filled him with joy he didn't know he could feel again.

Chad couldn't resist pulling her into his arms. He needed to feel her close to him, to reassure himself she really was awake and everything would be okay. She stiffened – but only for a moment, then she let him hold her.

"This feels familiar," she finally whispered. The crack in her voice tore at him, but at least he was hearing her speak.

"I'm so glad you're awake," he said without thinking.

"How long have I been asleep?"

Chad tensed. He didn't know if he should answer that. The doctor said to keep her calm.

"Please tell me," she pled.

"Two months," he answered and watched the color drain from her face once more. "It will be okay, Bree," he quickly assured, tugging her close again.

Bree felt the walls closing in on her. She'd been asleep for months and didn't remember anything. How could that happen to a person? She felt an overwhelming need to get out of there. She fought back the tears wanting to escape. She somehow knew she wasn't that kind of woman, she wouldn't lose control.

He gently rubbed her back, calming her, and she took a deep breath. She couldn't change the past so she had to move forward. Little did she know how many more shocks were coming her way. She felt exhaustion begin to overtake her again and didn't understand how she could be so tired when she'd been asleep for months.

"What happened?" she finally asked. She had to know.

"We need to wait for the doctor and your family," he said. He wasn't going to be responsible for giving her any more information that could jeopardize her health.

"Please, I need to know," she tried, but he stood firm. He needed to find out what information was safe to give to her, and what wasn't. He wouldn't do anything else to cause her further harm.

Dr. Bailey stepped in the room, saving him. She turned her eyes on him.

"Good to see you awake again, Bree," he said as he walked over and checked her charts.

"I need answers. Why am I here?" She got right to the point.

Dr. Bailey sat in a chair next to her bed and looked her over for a few moments before speaking.

"I think that's a discussion for you to have with your family. I'm here to tell you, your health looks good. If you can eat some solid food and work hard over the next week, we can let you get out of here," he answered, avoiding her question.

"But why am I here in the first place," she asked, her voice cracking even more in her frustration.

"Your family will fill you in on all of that, but I do have some great news for you. It's the reason you need to focus on eating so you can leave here," Dr. Bailey said. Chad tensed. He didn't want the doctor to blurt out the news, but the man was either ignoring him, or disregarding what he wanted.

"What?" Bree asked, momentarily distracted.

"You're about eight weeks pregnant."

There was pure silence as the news sank in. Bree's startled eyes went from the doctor to Chad, who managed to muster up an encouraging smile.

"I… I…" Bree couldn't seem to find words.

"It will all be okay, Bree," Chad said, though he didn't know how to make anything okay. Bree had lost her memory, there were still unknown men after her, and he didn't know how to fight an unseen force.

Her hand glided to her stomach and he watched as tears flashed in her eyes.

"Ours?"

"Yes," he answered with zero hesitation. She gave him a tentative smile, and all her other questions were forgotten as she pondered the reality of impending motherhood.

Chapter Eight

"After your ultrasound, if everything is fine with the baby, you'll be free to leave," Dr. Bailey said before Bree was able to open her mouth.

She'd come out of her coma two weeks ago but was still confined to her hospital room. Okay, not exactly the room, she was allowed to walk to the cafeteria, and even sit outside on occasion – as long as she had someone with her, but still, being stuck in a hospital, even a nice one, made her feel trapped.

She'd been a good sport about it for the first week and a half, but then her irritation at the situation became quite apparent to everyone. She was now used to the revolving door of visitors who called themselves her family, though she still hadn't gotten her memory back, but she just wanted to leave. She didn't know where home was, but anything had to be better than the sterile hospital room.

"Looks like he knows you well," Chad said with a laugh. Bree shot him a glare, and then regretted it. Chad was the one person she felt 'right' being around. She figured they must be incredibly close, because when he walked in the door, she felt butterflies in her stomach. He stirred things inside her she couldn't fully comprehend.

She thought she may be falling in love with him – though she had to love him already if they'd made a baby, right? She hated to start having those thoughts because they made her head hurt trying to put the pieces together of her broken memory.

"You promise?" she asked the doctor, ignoring Chad's comment.

"I promise – but only if the ultrasound says everything is good," he reminded her. She refused to think anything could be wrong.

She hadn't felt the baby move, didn't show any signs of pregnancy yet, but still, she had a connection to her unborn baby. Being pregnant gave her hope that her endless blank of a mind would have to someday clear.

She had a huge, obviously loving family, who visited her every day. And she couldn't define Chad. He was by her side night and day, and he was just so… She couldn't even put into words what he was.

Masculine.

Charming.

Manly.

Handsome.

There were thousands of descriptions, she was sure could describe him better.

"I'm ready," she said, excited to see the first images of her baby. Maybe seeing the pictures would stimulate her brain somehow and she'd regain her memory. She secretly crossed her fingers.

Another person came in the room, pushing a table with a machine and large monitor on it. She felt her nerves flutter at the sight. She was moments away.

Chad sat silently by Bree's bedside as he watched the hospital staff move around her room. He'd been on combat missions where he hadn't shed a single drop of sweat, but waiting to see the first images of his unborn child was like sitting in a hole anticipating the first grenade to drop. He was terrified something could be wrong with the baby, but overjoyed to see his son or daughter.

Without thought he reached out and gripped Bree's hand. She grew stronger each day and he hoped his child did too. She tensed at the coldness of the gel placed on her stomach, but soon there was a fuzzy image on the screen.

They both watched intensely as the technician moved the small wand around her belly, stopping every few seconds and clicking buttons on his monitor. Chad wanted to strangle the guy and demand he tell them everything was going to be all right.

Chad looked on, but couldn't see anything even sort of resembling a person inside her. Was something wrong? He had to fight not to shout.

"I'm just getting a few pictures of the womb right now. Your baby is very small at this point. Not even the size of a shelled peanut, and there's a lot of fluid and other internal things in the way, so it's hard to catch a good shot, but give me a moment longer," the guy finally spoke. It was a good thing, because Chad didn't think he could take much more silence.

The doctor bent down and looked at a place on the monitor where the technician had paused. They both spoke quietly for a moment and Chad felt a bead of sweat run down his brow. He was startled by how intense his emotions were. He'd never thought it possible to love something so much that he hadn't even known he wanted.

"You both will be pleased to know the baby is developing exactly as it should at this point in the pregnancy. This first machine gave us valuable information we needed. Now, Henry is hooking up our three dimensional ultrasound. Your baby is in a great position, so you're going to get a fairly clear image of him. At ten weeks along, your child is about an inch long and weighs less than an ounce," Dr. Bailey explained.

They both let out relieved breaths at the doctor's words. Bree turned toward Chad and sent him a stunning smile that would've dropped him to his knees had he not already been sitting. She had her color back and looked even more radiant than before. Pregnancy was beautiful on her – as was everything else.

"So, I can go home, right?" she asked.

"Yes. You're doing great. All signs point toward a full recovery and a healthy pregnancy," Dr. Bailey answered. He left out the amnesia. They didn't dwell on that as it would hopefully cure itself in time.

"Here's your baby," he said and they turned back to the screen. Before them was the image of their infant. It was obvious the baby was awake and moving around. Chad was dazed to see what looked like tiny arms moving in front of a large head. The image made it appear bigger than a peanut.

"Remember, this image is blown up, but your baby is almost fully developed. They grow rapidly at this stage of pregnancy. In a few weeks he, or she, will be fully formed, just have a lot of growing left to do. The first three months of pregnancy move the fastest in terms of development," Dr. Bailey informed them. Neither could take their eyes from the screen and they only absently nodded at his words. It was amazing to watch the tiny babe moving inside her body.

"Would you like to hear the heartbeat now?"

"Yes." They both answered in unison and then smiled at each other.

Chad was already filled with unbelievable love for his son or daughter, but when the sound of its already beating heart filled the room, he thought his own would burst. Such a strong sound for something so tiny.

Bree wasn't ready for the flood of love and protectiveness that washed through her. She couldn't remember a thing about her life, but it didn't matter. None of it did. Before her was the image of the life she carried within her, and the room was filled with the strong sound of its beating heart. Chad was holding her hand – she felt complete. Her stress drained away and she wanted to stay in the moment for as long as possible.

"Because of the medical conditions, I want to see you next week. If everything is still going great, we'll go to every two weeks for a couple months. I want to see you a bit more than normal, just to make sure you and your baby stay healthy and safe. If you can promise me that, I'll sign your release forms," Dr. Bailey offered.

Bree quickly agreed. She would sign away anything just to leave – but she wanted to keep an eye on the baby, too, so agreeing to extra doctor visits wasn't a hardship.

Dr. Bailey left them alone to get their emotions under control, while the technician printed them their first pictures of their child.

"Thank you, Bree. Thank you for this gift," Chad told her once they were alone. Bree looked at him and felt her heart flutter. She had so many questions, but none of them mattered in that moment. She slowly stood up, anxious to get dressed, when Chad surprised her by coming around the side of the bed and lifting her off the ground in a spine shattering hug.

She didn't even think about resisting him, she wanted his arms around her. She wanted more – so much more. Chad loosened his grip, but didn't release her. All of a sudden they were standing chest to chest, their faces only inches apart, and Bree's breath hitched again. Not from nerves or fear, but from pure excitement.

She could fully understand how she'd gotten pregnant. Her stomach tightened with need, desire racing through her blood.

She watched as Chad's eyes darkened, answering the need in her own face. She felt the pressure on her stomach as his need made itself known to her, pressing against her softness. The knowledge that she'd made this stronger than life man hard, caused her knees to tremble. She let out a moan without realizing it, and Chad quickly closed the gap between them.

As his lips brushed against hers, Bree moaned again. Sensation washed through her body as he molded his mouth against hers. She readily opened to his seeking tongue, and felt storm clouds building inside her.

She pushed against his hardness, feeling power when he trembled against her. She was turning this strong man to a quivering mass. She wanted more – wanted to make him cry out, like he was making her.

She ran her hands up his solid arms, raking her short nails against his tan skin. She reached his neck and would've smiled had her lips not been occupied, when she felt bumps appear on his skin. He deepened the kiss, thrusting his tongue far inside the recesses of her mouth.

Chad moved his hands to the back of her hospital gown, easily slipping inside the paper-thin robe. She shuddered as his large hands made contact with her bare skin. More. She had to have all of him.

She lost complete control and didn't care. She was safe. She was wanted. She was needed. She loved him, she somehow just knew it.

Chad reached down to lift her in his arms, having every intention of setting her on the hard hospital bed and taking her right there, when a knock on the door stopped him cold. It was better than an icy shower.

He quickly shielded Bree's body, to give her time to get her gown back in place as the door opened.

"Are you decent, Honey?" George asked as he cracked the door. "The doctor said I just missed the ultrasound but that you had some pictures for me."

George stepped in and looked from Chad's flushed face to Bree's shaking form behind him, and quickly put two and two together.

"I'm sorry to interrupt. I'll just wait out here for you," he said as he started to close the door. Bree was mortified to have been caught necking, by her father, nonetheless – even if she didn't remember him being her dad. She did know he loved her – as he'd been at the hospital almost as much as Chad.

"It's okay d… dad," she stammered. She still tripped on the name, but felt wrong calling him George. He'd told her it was all right if she needed to, but he'd said it with suspiciously moist eyes. "We just finished the ultrasound and Chad was just getting ready to leave so I can get dressed," she finished. She was bright red as she said the words, but George let her get away with the lie.

"I'll wait outside with your father," Chad said. His entire body was on fire, and he knew he was going to have a difficult time walking, but she needed a few minutes to compose herself and get dressed. He'd been hoping to help her dress… after he'd gotten rid of the gown and sunk himself deep inside her.

He tried to rid himself of those thoughts. It wasn't helping his situation, and really not helping the pain in his lower body. He shifted as he stood awkwardly

next to George. He really needed to get her alone –
and in a bed.

"We'll be right outside, then," George answered
with a smile before stepping back out the door.

"I don't think it gets more embarrassing than
that," Bree said with a small laugh.

"It could have if he'd been two minutes later,"
Chad said. He laughed as he saw the horror dawn on
her face. Then he stepped through the doors and
leaned his head against the cool metal. He couldn't
seem to keep it together around her. He was
beginning to think that wasn't such a bad thing.

Chapter Nine

"I don't like it," Trenton said with his arms folded across his chest. It seemed everyone was against him on the matter, though.

"I think it's safest. The doctor said she shouldn't be forced into anything, plus this way Chad can still keep a watch on her," George argued.

"He doesn't seem to be doing such a great job," he snapped, instantly regretting his words because he knew Chad was eating himself up about Bree getting hurt. It wasn't Chad's fault Bree had been shot. "I'm sorry. That was uncalled for," he quickly added.

"I understand," Chad replied. He would've gladly taken that bullet, but they couldn't dwell on it. They had no choice but to move forward, and at that moment they were discussing where Bree was going after her hospital release.

"Look, she's comfortable around me. I can look after her and my baby. Mark is only a couple miles away and you can camp in my back yard if you want," Chad said. He wanted Bree with him and wasn't compromising on the subject.

"It's not like he can get her any more pregnant," Mark added with a chuckle. Trenton shot daggers at his cousin.

"Like you're a monk," Alex added. Trenton felt they were teaming up against him. He didn't like it one bit.

"We're not discussing me," Trenton said, but he knew they were right. His sister wasn't a teenager anymore. He figured the protective feelings just never went away. He felt like Chad was taking advantage of the situation.

"Listen, I understand how you feel. But you have to realize at some point that Bree is an adult and she wasn't hurt when she made the decision to sleep with me. She's carrying my child. That means something to me. I plan on marrying her."

"Besides, her memory will come back, and if she's at home when it happens, there's going to be hell to pay. She'll accuse us of taking advantage of the situation, then we could lose her permanently. I think she needs to stay with Chad for now. He'll keep her safe," Austin jumped in.

Trenton reluctantly nodded his head but it was obvious he wasn't happy about the situation.

"Now that we got that settled, we should stop fighting before Bree turns the corner and wonders what it's all about. It wouldn't do her recovery any good to know she's got a stalker," George reminded them.

Within a few minutes, Bree joined them in the waiting area. She had a tentative smile on her face as she glanced toward the door, obviously wanting to exit the hospital before the doctor changed his mind and told her she couldn't leave.

"Let's get out of here, shall we?" Chad said, placing his arm around her back. She looked a bit lost, but was more than happy to follow him from the sterile room.

"We haven't discussed where I'm going. I don't even know where I live," Bree said, starting to feel her first stirrings of panic. It was disorienting to not know anything about her life.

"We're going home," Chad simply answered.

"Do we live together?"

"Yes," he answered somewhat truthfully. He had been staying with her so it wasn't exactly a lie. He had a feeling it was going to come back and bite him later, but he'd deal with that then.

"Okay," she said, seeming unsure, but putting her trust in him, anyway.

"We'll meet you at the ranch," George said before giving Bree a quick hug.

"Don't you think you all should wait a day or two before overwhelming her?" Chad asked. His question was ignored as everyone headed for their vehicles. They already had a welcome home party planned, and whether Bree was ready or not, she was about to be inundated with family.

Chad helped Bree into his truck, then went around and climbed into the driver's seat. He turned the radio to a country station and quietly started navigating the vehicle, letting her get used to the idea of finally being free from what she considered a prison.

"How far away is the house?"

"It's about a half hour from the hospital."

"Do I like living in the country?"

"I just bought this property. Before you went into the hospital, we were staying in a small house on the outskirts of town. I think you'll really enjoy the ranch, though. We have horses, cows, chickens, goats, and a few other creatures running around," he answered, his voice filled with excitement.

Bree felt a stirring of familiarity at his words. Maybe she'd spent time on a ranch before. She started to feel excitement as they left the city and glided past fields of hay, gently blowing in the breeze.

It didn't seem like much time passed when Chad turned off the main road and started traveling down a long gravel driveway. Her head turned from side to side as she tried to take in everything around her. She looked out at the fruit trees and could practically feel the burst of flavor on her tongue. She knew she'd spent time climbing apple trees and plucking fruit from their branches. She just didn't know when she'd done it.

They turned a bend in the road and her eyes widened at the number of cars lined up in front of a huge three story home. She heard Chad curse and turned in his direction.

"I told your family to take it easy and let you get adjusted first, but they don't seem to listen. It was only supposed to be immediate family members but it looks like they brought the entire gang. If you want me to turn around and take you to a hotel for the night, I will," he offered when he saw her frightened expression.

"No, I'll be okay. It's obvious my family loves me, which is great. It's better to be overwhelmed, than have nobody at all," she answered. Chad would see if she still felt that way in a few hours.

"You're home! I'm so glad you're okay," Jennifer said as she rushed up and threw her arms around Bree as soon as she stepped from the vehicle.

"Aunt Bree, I missed you," Molly cried out as she ran up to them and joined in on the hug.

"I missed you, too," Bree automatically answered. She hugged both of them, though she still didn't recognize anyone. She was then passed from one pair of arms to the next for several minutes. It brought tears to her eyes, all the love she was receiving. She seemed to be a very lucky person.

"We have the steaks going, cousin. Come sit down and relax for a while," Mark said when she finally made it into the house. She looked around the large entrance with sparse furnishings.

"Come out back, Sweetie. We have a nice chair all set up for you," Joseph called in a voice that made Bree jump. She knew he was her uncle, but the man was a bit intimidating. He was as huge as a mountain, with a voice that could easily command an army.

"Joseph, you're scaring the poor girl. Let her get settled," Esther said as she came up and put her arm around Bree.

"Nonsense. My niece would never be afraid of me," Joseph protested.

"Humph," Esther replied before whisking Bree away. Bree had to admit she was grateful for the woman's interference.

"I'm sorry, this is all just a little overwhelming," Bree admitted quietly to the kind woman leading her to a secluded space in the back yard.

"It's alright, dear. Your family means well, and they love you deeply, but sometimes they can be a bit much to handle," Esther said with a knowing wink.

"It seems that way."

"I'm Esther. I've worked for the Anderson's for many years. I'm retired now but they've become so much a part of my family, that I can't seem to stay away," she said with a gentle laugh. Bree felt completely at ease with her.

"It seems they wouldn't let you go, even if you wanted to leave," Bree said with wide eyes as she looked over the yard filled with people, young and old, all of them laughing and carrying on. She smiled as she saw a couple toddlers on one end of a see-saw and Chad on the other side. He was shooting them into the air, sending them into fits of contagious laughter.

Bree felt a flash of memory register. She saw herself flying high on a swing with Jasmine next to her, both of them laughing. Bree smiled, then giggled, overcome with happiness at the small piece of her past. For the first time since waking from her coma, she felt like it really was her family.

Chad looked over and their eyes connected, sending a bolt of electricity zipping through the air. Her stomach clenched with need so overwhelming she had to quickly sit because she didn't think her legs would carry her weight any longer. When she saw the instant heat in Chad's eyes, it caused her body to go from hot to smoldering. She instantly wished they were alone. Maybe when she was once again in his arms, it would flood her mind with her life before the accident. She suddenly wanted to have her memories back more than anything. It seemed she had a very fulfilled life.

"Higher," the kids on the see-saw called to him, impatient with his momentary pause. He jerked his gaze from hers and started playing with them again. Bree realized she'd stopped breathing and took in a fortifying breath of air.

***

"Do you see the heat flying between those two?" George asked his brother with a satisfied smile.

"I'm surprised the dry grass doesn't ignite," Joseph confirmed.

"I hate that my daughter has been through so much, but I'm sure glad Chad was the one to step into her life. I think another wedding may be in the near future," George beamed.

"I'm happy for you, brother. You deserve joy in your life. Speaking of which, I think I've detected some sparks between you and Esther," Joseph said with a twinkle in his eye.

"Now, don't you start matchmaking on me. Esther and I are only friends," George said in a hushed tone as he looked around, making sure no one had overheard them. If his kids even suspected he had feelings for Esther, they'd be all over him. He knew they had their own suspicions about Joseph and him stepping into their children's lives and matchmaking.

"I'm just saying…" Joseph trailed off. He watched as George's eyes sought out Esther every few minutes or so. It looked to him like his brother may have found a second chance of happiness in life. He deserved it. Losing his wife was devastating for him, and Esther was a good woman.

"Well, don't you be saying anything. And don't even think about getting any fool idea's in your head," George said before he stomped off to speak to someone else. Joseph's loud laughter followed him across the yard.

***

"My Dad and Esther, huh? I would've never even imagined it," Austin said to his cousin, Lucas.

"Eavesdropping definitely has its benefits," Lucas said as he watched his uncle stomp away.

"He's mourned long enough. I think it would be great if he was able to find someone to grow old with," Austin said.

"I just think it's time he gets paid back. I can't prove it, but I know Dad and Uncle George have been meddling in our lives. They think they're so slick, but they start crying about grandkids and all of a sudden they have more than a houseful. That seems like more than just a coincidence to me," Trenton mused.

"Good thing I'm smarter than the rest of you," Austin answered smugly.

"Sure, Cuz, we'll see how smart you are," Trenton laughed. Austin glared at his cousin before walking away.

"What are you two up to?" Jennifer asked as she came up and wrapped her arms around her husband.

"Looks like Dad may be falling in love. We think it's time to do some interfering of our own," Trenton answered, quickly kissing his wife. He couldn't seem to get enough of her, no matter how much time he spent at her side.

"What do you mean?" she asked, looking confused.

"I don't know how the old men have done it, but I know they've been meddling in our love lives. Not that I'm complaining – it led me to you," Trenton added. He loved his wife and wouldn't change a thing between them.

"Then why do you want revenge?"

"Not revenge, my dear - payback," he said with a twinkle in his eye.

"Men," she said before kissing him and heading back to the other women, who made far more sense. Trenton enjoyed watching her as she walked away. The longer he was with her, the more he fell in love. She only grew more beautiful each day.

***

"How are you holding up?" George asked.

"I'm still standing," Bree answered. She didn't think any of them planned on leaving the ranch anytime soon. They'd all been there for several hours and the party was in full bloom. She was tired, but didn't want to admit her weakness to them. She had a feeling she wasn't normally one to complain about things.

"I'll start rounding everyone up. They're just so excited to have you back home," George said.

"You don't have to do that, I'm fine," she automatically responded. She felt as if she were ungrateful, when everyone had been nothing but kind to her.

"It's okay to be tired, Bree. You've been through a lot. Your brothers have always been protective over you, and the years of lost time when everyone mourned the loss of your mother has made them even more so. Too much time was lost, and now we all want to be reassured that nothing will rip our family apart again," he explained.

Bree loved him – she couldn't remember him being her father, but he was such a kind and gentle man, and she knew beyond a doubt that she loved him. She threw her arms around him and clung for several moments. When she pulled back, there were tears in his eyes.

"Thank you, Dad. I'm sure everything will eventually come back to me, but one thing I know is that I love you. I can feel it in my heart, even if my mind is shut down at the moment."

"That's the best thing you could ever say to me. I love you, too, Sweetheart. Now, I'm going to get all these testosterone filled men out of here so you can get off your feet and rest. You are growing my beautiful grandchild, after all."

Bree laughed as she let him take her arm and lead her to the porch. She thought a nap sounded pretty heavenly right then, though. She was passed around once again as everyone said goodbye. The little kids all needed a hug and kiss from her, and she once again felt that warm glow in her heart as she held them tightly against her chest. She obviously loved this big chaotic family. Memory or not, she felt at home – at ease with her world.

She stood next to Chad as they waved goodbye to the last departing family members.

"Sorry about that, Bree. When your family makes up their minds, there's no stopping them. That's one of the things I love about them most," Chad told her as he led her inside. Bree collapsed in the comfortable chair, feeling like her eye lids weighed fifty tons.

"I loved it. They're a bit overwhelming, but it's obvious they love me. I think my memory will come back. I have a good feeling about it…" she trailed off.

Her words sent an arrow of panic through Chad. When she realized he'd lied to her, she was going to be furious. He would just make sure she fell in love with him before that happened so she wouldn't want to leave.

"That's great. I need to go tend the animals," he said, sounding short as he strode out the door. He tried to ignore the startled look in her eyes, and the flash of hurt his words caused. He mucked the horse stalls until his muscles were screaming and sweat dripped from his brow. He pushed himself hard, hoping by the time he went inside, he'd be able to fall face first into bed and pass out.

It didn't work. After a hot shower, he crawled into bed, where he laid for hours, his mind filled with thoughts of Bree, and wishing she were lying next to him. He would've most likely caved and went to her, had she not been sleeping so soundly.

She wanted her own room until she felt more comfortable in their relationship. She'd laughed about it, patting her stomach, but she said it felt wrong for them to sleep together when he was too much like a stranger still. Though he may not survive it, he hadn't argued with her. But he didn't think he was going to get any rest with her sleeping only a few short feet away.

Chapter Ten

Chad took a deep breath and squared his shoulders. He wanted to marry her, and preferably before she got her memory back. She carried his child – he wouldn't let the baby be raised without a father. He'd be there to always protect them both.

Bree was sitting in the kitchen when he came around the corner. She gave him a tentative smile, unsure of why he'd stormed away from her the night before.

"Let's get married now," he blurted, then wished he could take back his words when her eyes widened and she sat with a stunned look on her face. He should have gently approached the subject.

He could see a myriad of thoughts running through her mind. He knew she thought he was probably insane. Hot, then cold. She wouldn't know what to think.

"Did we discuss marriage before the accident?" she asked, not taking her eyes from his. He could lie but he wouldn't go that far.

"No, but things were good between us."

"I don't want a marriage of convenience. I know, I don't know how, but I know I can only marry for love. I can barely comprehend being pregnant, and I wish I had my memory back, but I'm not going to marry you just because we slept together. Every time I ask you about the past, you hedge around it. Why?"

"The doctor said not to force anything on you."

"That's a cop-out and you know it," she replied, getting irritated with him.

"It's the truth," he insisted.

"Would you have asked me to marry you if I wasn't pregnant?"

Chad stood there like a deer caught in headlights. All he needed to say was 'yes' but he knew it was a lie. Maybe eventually he would've asked her, he tried to reason with himself. But he'd always vowed never to get married. Having a baby changed things, though. They needed to put the needs of their child's welfare ahead of themselves. She should understand that.

"That question doesn't matter – it's irrelevant," he hedged.

"I disagree. I think it's completely relevant."

"I want to raise my child. Does that make me a bad guy?"

"You can be active in your child's life without marrying me. I don't even know you, not really. Maybe I'll feel differently once my memories come back, but you're not helping matters by acting like a Neanderthal," she scolded.

"You're my responsibility. I don't shirk on what's right."

"So, now I'm nothing more than a responsibility. One more daily chore for you to take care of."

"You're twisting my words," he huffed in frustration. Chad moved around the room, running his fingers through his hair, trying to figure out how to get through to her. Why did she have to be so stubborn?

He walked to the fridge and started pulling items out. He had to do something with his hands or he feared he may place them around her small neck and strangle her. He smirked at himself. He would never, in a million years, hurt a woman. He wanted to kill the men who'd dare to harm her. Until they were caught, she was still in danger. If she'd just agree to marry him, he could protect her and the baby. Even with amnesia, she was pure Anderson, stubborn, even to the point of self-sacrifice.

Chad tossed a sandwich in front of her, then sat at the table and took a large bite of his sandwich. He was angry – and she was frustrated.

"Maybe I should just go and stay with my father. I think he'd like that."

"No."

"You can't just tell me no. I'm an adult, in case you haven't noticed," she said with a glare.

"You'll stay here," he commanded. He was really ticking her off.

"You insufferable pig. Don't you dare try to tell me what to do!" she snapped, standing up so fast her chair went flying behind her.

Chad jumped from his seat at the same time. He was furious with himself – the stalker – the situation – just about everything. He tried to calm himself down – remember she'd only been home one day.

"I'm going to the barn," he said, turning to leave. He was proud of the restraint he was able to use. His passion always flared whenever he was in the same room with her, hell, within the same county.

"Afraid of a girl? Or is it that you just can't handle it when a female doesn't fall all over herself trying to please you. I bet you're used to men, women, and children bowing all over themselves to do your bidding," she said, then turned to make what she hoped was a dramatic exit. Men!

Chad sent her a smoldering look that was wasted on her retreating back.

"What? Does Princess Bree not like someone disagreeing with her? You have it all backwards, Honey. I think you're the one who's so used to getting her own way, she can't handle it when she doesn't get the last word in, or win the argument."

Bree had never in her life wanted to punch someone, but she felt her fists curling as she fought the urge to walk back and slug him in his smug mouth. He was calling her a princess. She looked around his impressive home with a derisive laugh. Sure, she'd learned she came from money, but he didn't look to be hurting, himself.

"I'm sorry. It doesn't look as if you like that. Would you like for me to get on one knee and beg for forgiveness?" he said with a grin.

"That works just fine for me," she answered.

"Good luck with that," he snarled.

"I'm leaving," she answered and took a single step before he grabbed her arm and whipped her around to face him.

"I don't understand what it is you do to me, but I can't resist you – not even for your own good," he growled before grabbing a handful of her hair and pulling her against his body. His head dropped and his mouth connected with the sweet heaven of her lips.

Bree's eyes widened as anger turned into full-blown passion, but her body knew what she wanted, and she quickly clutched at his shirt, opened her mouth, and held on for dear life.

Bree instantly melted as he seduced her with his hands and mouth. The man could literally kiss the sense right out of her. She didn't care that they hadn't solved anything. She was hungry for him, and only he could feed her desire.

His body felt like steel underneath her hands. She wanted to feel skin against skin. Her nipples were painfully hard as they pressed into the lace of her bra. She needed the clothing gone – there were too many layers in her way.

She moved her hands to his shirt and tugged at the material, wanting to run her fingers along the contours of his masculine chest – down the washboard that was his stomach, and lower to his hardness, currently pressing tightly into her stomach.

Chad took the hint and moved an inch back so he could rip his shirt off, then in the next second stripped hers and tossed it somewhere behind them. His hands moved back to her hair, tugging her close, causing her to cry out in pleasure.

"More – I need more," she cried as his hands moved to her neck, then lower to unclasp her bra. She breathed a sigh of relief when the cool evening air hit her aching nipples, then gasped in ecstasy as his mouth surrounded the tight pink bud of one, then the other. It felt so good, it was almost painful.

His teeth clamped down on her sensitive bud, making her back arch, and a guttural groan escape her dry throat. He swept his tongue along the well-loved skin, then moved back up the smooth column of her throat and she greedily bit down on his lip. He groaned and she felt her body heat rise to another level.

Chad stripped her pants and panties in one smooth motion, then lifted her up on the counter without breaking their mouths apart. She rubbed her nipples against his solid chest, trying to relieve the aching. It only stoked the flames higher.

"Now," she commanded him. She needed their bodies connected – she had to feel him inside her, or she'd die of sexual frustration.

"Can't wait anymore," Chad groaned as he parted her thighs, stepping between them. Bree barely caught a glimpse of his impressive manhood before his head was pushing against her tight entrance.

"Yes," she called as he pushed slightly inside her. He stalled and she raked her fingers down his back to his firm butt and pulled him closer. With a groan, he finally pushed inside her, and Bree saw lights going off behind her closed eyelids.

So full – so very full.

She felt complete as he filled every inch of her, stretching her in the very best way. She thought she couldn't possibly feel any better than she did in that moment – until he began moving.

Chad began thrusting in and out of her, slow at first, but quickly increasing his speed. Bree could do nothing but hold on tight as their bodies slid together, building up pressure, until finally she exploded in a fusion of light. She shook around him as he pumped inside her a few more times, before his body locked tightly against her and he quivered underneath her touch.

His hot breath skimmed across her neck as he leaned into her, shudders consuming him. She ran her fingers down his spine, his skin hot to the touch. He gently nipped her shoulder, then brushed his tongue across the point, alleviating any pinch. She didn't want to let go. She felt more emotion locked in his arms, than she had since waking from her coma. She didn't want to let the feeling go.

"Are you okay?" he asked.

"Better than okay. I don't know if I'm going to be able to move for at least a month," she sighed.

"Let me help you with that," he said lazily as he picked her up, their bodies still one, and carried her to his room. She tensed as she looked at his huge bed, wondering if it was too intimate of a step for her to climb in with him.

As her body tensed, she gripped his manhood, still hard within her, and caused another groan to escape him.

"No other woman has ever done this to me," he groaned as his body lit on fire once more. He laid them on the bed together with her locked tightly in his arms and started moving inside her still quivering body.

It didn't take her long to feel the pressure building back up, and soon all her worries were forgotten, at least for a little while.

***

Bree gulped down large sips of icy cold water. She finished one glass, then quickly polished off another. As she stood by the sink hydrating her body, she couldn't help but laugh.

She'd spent an entire day in bed with Chad, making love over and over again. She was surprised and delighted at how well he knew her body, inside and out. Between making love, she'd managed to catch a little sleep, but hadn't minded when he woke her, only to send her flying again.

He was an incredible lover, and she had to fight not to shout out, *yes, oh, yes, I'll marry you, anytime*. Lust and love weren't the same thing.

She ran her hand over her stomach and smiled. It was obvious they had no problem in the bedroom, but she didn't know how well they could do outside of it. He'd remained by her side the entire time she'd been in the hospital so that meant something, but still...

Bree turned off the water and stood for a moment, unsure what she should do. Chad was in the shower and they hadn't discussed if she was spending the night in his room. She would assume he wanted her there, considering they hadn't been able to tear themselves away from each other all day, but what if he wanted her to go to her own room now.

"I'm being stupid," she muttered out loud, then jumped at the sound of her own voice, causing her to giggle.

She heard the shower turn off and decided to stay where she was. She wanted to go to his bed, but at the same time, she wanted him to seek her out. There was nothing wrong with maintaining her pride, even if she'd let go of every ounce of self-control that day, already.

She looked out the window and noticed movement in the backyard. She didn't really think anything of it since the ranch was surrounded by animals. It most likely was one of his dogs, or maybe even a large raccoon. But something just seemed off.

The full moon illuminated the area and the barn light was casting eerie shadows across the ground. A shiver ran down her spine and she leaned in closer to the window. Once she assured herself it was nothing more than an animal she'd rest easier.

She didn't see anything further, so decided she'd just made a mountain out of a mole hill. It had to have been a shadow. The wind was whipping through the area. It was most likely a branch blowing. She was about to turn when another movement caught her eye. Something was giving her the creeps enough that she couldn't turn her eyes away from the spot.

She pressed closer to the cold glass, goosebumps appearing on her skin. Something was out there. An animal – it had to be an animal. She was ready to go to the back door so she could get a better look, when a cloud moved and she got a clearer vision of the backyard.

It was a person.

Someone was standing near the barn – looking right through the window at her. Bree made eye contact and felt a shudder ripple through her. She was so shocked; she stood motionless for several moments – until he took a menacing step in her direction.

She opened her mouth and screamed.

Chapter Eleven

Chad was putting the towel around his waist when he heard Bree's cry. He immediately jumped into action, instinct taking over.

He grabbed his gun without stopping as he ran from the room and raced around the corner, leading him into the kitchen where he found Bree staring out the window, her body shaking.

"A man – there's a man out there, and he's staring at me," she cried.

"Get down, now!" Chad commanded. The authority in his voice overrode the fear coursing through her and she dropped to the kitchen floor.

Chad hit the light switch over the stove, dropping the kitchen into darkness, making it easier for him to see outside.

"What's going on?" Bree whispered as she spotted the large gun Chad was carrying.

"I don't know," he responded, but he could see she didn't believe him. She stayed silent, though as he slowly popped up and glanced out the window.

"It may be nothing, but I swear he was looking right at me," she whispered, her voice thick with fear.

"Bree, I need you to crawl into the hallway. There are too many windows here and if this is a robber and he shoots, I don't want you getting hit by the glass," Chad once again commanded. He watched as Bree did as he asked.

Then, he went to the counter and picked up his phone.

"Get over here, now," he said into the device before quickly hanging up. She didn't know who he'd called, but obviously they didn't need more explanation than that.

Bree watched wide-eyed as Chad slowly popped up and looked out the window. He kept his body to the side, with only a portion of his head in the window while he searched the yard.

"Where did you see him?"

"Over by the barn."

"You're sure it was a man?"

"Yes, I locked eyes with him. It was definitely a man," she said with confidence.

"He may have moved closer to the house, or your scream might have scared him away. I'm still not taking any chances. Go into the bathroom and lock the door. I don't care what you hear; do not open that door. Underneath the vanity, feel around, there's a secret door, and inside you'll find a gun. Take it out. If anyone comes through that door, shoot first, ask questions later. I won't come in without knocking and letting you know it's me," he told her.

"I don't understand. Secret gun compartments? Crazy stalkers? What is going on?"

"We don't have time right now, please, just do what I asked," he commanded. Bree scooted away to the end of the hall and waited on the other side. She wasn't quite ready to head to the bathroom.

She poked her head around and watched as Chad flipped on the back porch light and looked through the window. She saw him staring out it, looking in every direction. He moved to the back door and looked through that as well. It didn't seem real, with him standing there in nothing but a towel, holding a deadly looking black gun in his hand, with all the lights off inside.

Then the first shot rang out, seeming to echo through the house. The kitchen window shattered and Bree felt her face drain of any color that might have been left. She decided it was time to listen, and scrambled to the bathroom, shutting and locking the door.

There was a night light casting shadows in the large room. Though there were no windows in it, she still crawled to the vanity, where she felt around for the secret compartment Chad spoke about.

It took her several minutes, but finally she found the latch and opened the small door, reached her hand inside and came out with the gun he spoke of. Her fingers shook as she took the weapon in her hand, then crawled over to the back wall and sat there huddled.

Please don't have to use this, please don't have to use this, she repeated over and over in her head. What if she fired it and hit Chad? What if she hit her own leg? She wasn't used to weapons and didn't know the first thing about how to fire a gun. She just hoped she wouldn't have to have her first lesson on a real live person.

***

Chad waited to hear the click from the bathroom door before he moved forward again. He didn't know where the guy was – didn't even know if he was alone, or had help. All he knew was that he wasn't going to let them near Bree again, not while he was still alive.

He glanced back out and caught a flash of light glinting off metal. It was an instant red flag and he quickly dropped to the ground as the gunshot rang out and slammed through the kitchen window.

He covered his head as the window shattered to his left, littering the kitchen floor with shards of glass. He kept his ears tuned toward the back of the house, making sure the door didn't open. Bree needed to stay out of there. He could hold them off, but he needed to know she was safe.

He crawled back from the door, wishing he would've put on some pants after his shower. He felt too vulnerable in nothing but a small swatch of cotton.

The next shot rang out and hit the stone columns on his porch. He knew he just had to wait them out. He wanted to rush into the yard, take down the bastards daring to shoot at his home, but he couldn't leave Bree. That was probably what they were hoping for.

Chad moved to the hallway as more bullets besieged the house. He listened for several moments, noticing a pattern to the shots. They were ringing out exactly two minutes apart. He waited, counting, and sure enough, the next shot came right on time.

As soon as the shot went off, he moved back toward the window and peaked into his yard. He saw the glint of metal from the trees near his barn. There was a slight movement, then exactly two minutes later, another shot rang out. Holy Hell! It wasn't a person firing. They had some sort of device set up. He needed to get to Bree.

He heard glass shattering in one of the back bedrooms and he immediately ran for that area. The gun was nothing but a diversion to keep him busy. The stalker was coming after her.

Chad's body tensed as he made his way down the hall, looking through each open doorway, before quickly passing by them. He reached the room he'd heard the glass breaking and looked inside. A man wearing a full black mask was looking right at him through the open window. Chad lifted his gun and fired a shot but the man ducked out of the way at the last minute.

He never popped back up and Chad was torn between chasing after him and ending the hunt for Bree, or staying in the house to keep her safe. If the guy had a partner and Chad left the house he'd never forgive himself.

"Chad, it's me," Mark called out as he rushed in through the front door, not even considering his own safety.

"Back here," Chad called, and he heard Mark's footsteps echoing down the hallway as he ran through the dark house.

"Where is he?" Mark demanded, his own weapon drawn.

"I just fired at him through the window. Bree's in the bathroom, watch her, I'm going after this guy," Chad said as he stepped forward to jump through the window. Mark grabbed his arm.

"The guys are on their way, along with the sheriff. Get some pants on and guard Bree. I'll go after him," Mark said before rushing toward the window.

Chad wanted to argue, but Mark was right. He needed to get some clothes on. He was too vulnerable in nothing but a towel.

"Fine," he grimaced as Mark jumped out the window.

Chad quickly moved into action and rushed to his room, where he threw on his pants, a pair of shoes and gun holster in less than twenty seconds. He didn't bother with a shirt, there was no time. He quickly rushed back to the window Mark had jumped out, and didn't see anything. He wanted to chase after him, but he wouldn't leave Bree.

"Chad," Trenton called. Chad changed directions and ran toward the front door.

"Right here," he answered so they'd know it was him. "Bree's in the bathroom. Knock and tell her who you are before opening the door. I told her to shoot first if anyone tried to enter," Chad warned as he rushed past Trenton and out the front door.

He stayed low to the ground as a shot rang out near his barn. He needed to get out there. He skirted the barn and came up behind the trees, looking in every direction, making sure he wasn't headed into an ambush.

Just as another shot rang out, he rounded the back of the barn and spotted the contraption firing at his house. Chad was filled with rage as he approached the rotating gun. He quickly disarmed it, trying to be careful not to touch too many areas, just in case they were able to pull prints from the weapon. He had a feeling the stalker was smart enough not to leave prints, though.

"Chad, get over here," Mark hollered.

Chad turned toward the sound of Mark's voice and jogged to the front of the house.

"What have you found?" Chad asked.

"I'm going to kill someone," Mark replied. Chad was surprised by his words. Mark was normally the mellowest guy he knew, though Chad knew his best friend could certainly be counted on. He was afraid to know what it was that had got him so riled up.

"They left this."

Chad turned to see a bloody doll on his front steps with a sign attached to it.

We got her once, we'll get her again.

"Who are these people," Chad shouted. He quickly calmed himself down. He had to stay strong, he couldn't afford to lose his composure.

***

Bree sat shivering in the bathroom. She heard the men shouting in the hallway. Trenton was there, along with Mark. She didn't know who else. She couldn't make herself move, though. She still clutched the gun in her hand, pointing it toward the door. Fear of any small movement would make her fire the dang thing, but she couldn't force her arms to lower the weapon.

She listened as footsteps ran up and down the hall, doors slammed, and voices shouted. What was going on? Who would want to harm them? Chad hadn't seemed surprised, confusing her even more. Why wouldn't he tell her if something was going on? Would he really be so stupid as to think she couldn't handle the information?

Considering she didn't really know what she could handle or not handle, maybe he was right not to tell her. The thoughts just kept running over themselves through her mind, leaving her in a constant state of terror as she waited for Chad to come back.

The worst part was the image of that man staring at her. She didn't think she'd ever get the picture of those deadly looking eyes from her mind. The moment had seemed to stretch on forever, their eyes locked together. A shiver ran down her spine.

Bree shut her eyes and shook her head, trying to dispel the man from her mind. Chad wouldn't let anything happen to her. She knew that – she somehow had complete faith in the man – faith that he'd never let harm come to her – not if he could help it.

Finally, the shots stopped firing. She hadn't realized she'd been counting them until the midnight silence. Ten shots – ten agonizing booms in the night. Each time the gun fired, she'd clenched, praying one of those deadly bullets didn't hit Chad.

The silence was almost worse than the exploding sound of bullets. She at least knew something was happening, could pinpoint where the danger was when there were shots fired. In the silence, she strained her ears, trying to pick up any sound.

What were they doing?

Why wasn't anyone coming to reassure her?

Were they dead?

She was terrified and hanging on by only a very short thread. She didn't care what Chad had told her to do. If someone didn't come soon, she was leaving the bathroom. She'd rather face the masked man than sit in the dark, not knowing, weak with trepidation.

"Bree, it's me, Trenton. I'm going to open the bathroom door now. You can put down the gun, okay?"

It took a couple of seconds for the words to process in her head. She stared at the doorknob as it slowly started to turn. Her arms never moved - the gun still aimed straight for whoever came through the opening.

"Bree, can you answer me. I'd prefer not to get shot," Trenton said with a nervous chuckle.

The door opened and he looked around the side of the door. She met his eyes; hers rounded in shock, the gun aimed toward him.

"Are you going to put the gun down, Bree? It's over. You're safe now."

She didn't move, didn't say a word, just looked at him blankly.

"Listen, sis, you're in shock. I need you to lower the gun. You don't even have to let go of it, just lower it. Then I'll come in and help you, okay?"

She couldn't make herself move. She told herself to do what he asked, but she couldn't make her muscles listen to her mind.

"Chad," Trenton called. He wasn't afraid of getting shot, but he didn't want Bree traumatized any more than she already was. She obviously wasn't coping, and if she did shoot at him, or actually hit him, she'd be filled with regret and sorrow.

Chad quickly came running through the house, arriving at the door and looking inside. Bree's eyes seemed to clear a fraction when she saw Chad standing there.

"It's okay, baby. I'm going to come in now, and I'd really appreciate it if you didn't shoot me," Chad said as if he were talking to a child. He slowly stepped into the bathroom and started walking to her. He stayed close to the wall, trying to keep out of range of the weapon, just in case her finger twitched and she accidentally shot it.

Upon reaching her, he quickly sat down. She turned her head and made eye contact with him, her body beginning to tremble in earnest.

"I'm going to take the gun now, okay?" he asked, reaching up and gently releasing her fingers from the weapon, sliding the gun across the floor to Trenton, who stood back and watched.

As soon as the weapon was taken away, her arms dropped and tears poured from her eyes.

"It's okay, we're all okay," Chad reassured her as he pulled her onto his lap and started rocking her. "You're fine, Bree. Your family is here, there's no sign of the shooter."

She fell against him as the shock turned into fear and she allowed herself to be rocked in his arms. Her own arms wound around his neck as he continued to rock her, running his fingers through her hair, giving her time to cry out her fear and confusion.

Finally, Chad stood with her cradled in his arms and walked from the bathroom. Trenton had turned on the house lights, casting the eerie shadows away. Chad went straight to his room, where he gently laid her on his bed, continually whispering soothing words in her ear.

"We'll make sure the area is secure," Trenton said. It was obvious Chad couldn't leave Bree right then. "The doctor is on his way."

The doctor showed up within a half hour and gave Bree a sleeping aid. Chad held her in his arms until the medicine did its job and she fell asleep. He let Trenton and Mark lock up the place, neither of them would leave. They'd make sure the house was safe while he made sure Bree was alright. He didn't want her to wake alone – not after the night she'd had.

Chapter Twelve

Bree woke up and stretched, a smile playing on her lips, as for one moment she blissfully forgot about the night before. She stretched her arms out and came into contact with solid muscles. She slowly turned her head and found herself staring into the piercing blue eyes of Chad.

She blinked, momentarily disoriented by the mesmerizing quality of his baby blues with thick black lashes. But as she leaned forward, the night's events came flooding back and her body tensed. How could she have forgotten, even for a moment?

Chad didn't say anything as she sat up. Bree slipped from the bed and padded over to the bathroom, quietly shutting the door behind her. She leaned her head against it, taking a few deep breaths.

She just needed a hot shower and a few minutes alone to put her thoughts in order. She nearly laughed at that idea, considering she'd love to have a slate of memories, instead of just the few new ones she'd obtained since waking in the hospital.

She climbed under the pulsing shower spray and it felt as if the water washed her worries down the drain. It was almost ironic how a nice shower could cleanse her mind and body. She stayed in long enough that she knew Chad would be getting worried, but she couldn't seem to drag herself out.

When she eventually climbed out and brushed her teeth in the steam filled room, she was grateful the mirror was fogged and she didn't have to look at her reflection. She was sure her face was gaunt, with dark circles underneath her eyes. It was a good thing Chad was too much of a gentleman to say anything about it.

Bree stepped out the door and found Chad lying in the same spot she'd left him. He watched her enter the room in his oversized robe she'd found hanging on the back of the door. She felt her spirits lift from the way his eyes narrowed in desire. It made her feel like a wanton woman instead of just a victim.

She walked toward the bed, her heart accelerating the closer she got to him. She wanted his hands all over her. She wanted answers about the night before, but her body needed him more. They could always talk later – hopefully, much later.

She leaned down - noticing his eyes never left her. They explored the opening of the robe, where only a hint of cleavage showed, then moved down to catch glimpses of her legs as they peaked out from the bottom of the oversized garment, exploring every inch of her.

He suddenly moved, causing her to tumble down on top of him. He didn't hesitate in kissing her. He was rough with urgency as he worked his fingers into her wet strands of hair, using it to pull her closer.

He quickly twisted their bodies so he was on top of her – trapping her beneath his solid mass of muscles as he continued to ravage her mouth. She reached up and gripped his shoulders, her nails digging into his flesh, overwhelmed by the desire consuming her.

There was an urgency in their lovemaking, as if they both felt they wouldn't survive if they couldn't join together. It felt dangerous, hot and explosive – and she wanted more.

She moved her hands down his back, scraping along his flesh as she reached for his bare ass. She gripped him, pulling him into the heat of her thighs as she pushed against him.

He moved back a few inches to tear open the robe so they could touch – flesh to flesh. His pulsing erection was cradled at the heart of her, but not penetrating. She jerked her hips, hoping he'd take the hint and bury himself deep inside her more than ready body.

Still, he only rocked his hips, sliding his solid flesh along the outside of her aching core. He brushed against her, causing her to cry out in both pain and pleasure.

"Take me," she demanded as she pulled her lips from his. He gave her a wicked smile and gave the slightest shake of his head, denying her.

Bree glared at him, her body on fire, needing completion. His touch was making her crazy.

She bent her head to his shoulder and nipped his skin, making him lean back and smile again. He thought he had all the power, but after a full day of lovemaking, she knew how to bring him to his knees.

She ran her tongue along his throat, before moving down his neck, causing him to arch up as he enjoyed the sensation of her exploring mouth. She circled his chest and took his nipple into her mouth and gently bit down, causing his stomach to tremble.

When he was putty in her hands, she easily pushed him over to his back, then didn't waste any time climbing on his upper thighs. She looked down into his lust filled eyes before she bent and kissed him again. Her lips ached to taste him while mating their tongues together.

He placed his hands on her hips, pulling her to him, trying to rub his manhood against her heat.

Finally!

She sat up, moving her hips forward so his swollen head was at her opening. Slowly, never taking her eyes from his, she slid down his hard staff, nearly exploding as he filled her up.

Chad's entire body tensed as she settled fully on him, her slick heat making it easy for them to slide together.

"You're the most stunning woman I've ever seen," he said with a groan as his eyes traveled down her throat, breasts and smooth stomach. She beamed at him before rising up, then quickly falling back down, loving every inch of him moving inside her.

Bree leaned forward as Chad raised his hands to cup her breasts. They bounced against his hands as she picked up her pace, moving steadily up and down his throbbing rod.

"Yes," she hissed when he pulled on her so he could take her nipple into his mouth. He teased the swollen peak mercilessly before he moved on to the other one. She rode him faster and faster as he loved on her breasts.

She sat up, the sensation almost becoming too much to bear. She leaned her hands on his legs behind her, giving her more leverage and picked up her pace once more. She was so close, ready for the explosion she knew was coming.

Chad reached his hand forward and flicked his fingers over her sensitive skin, sending her over the edge in a whirlwind of pleasure.

She sank against his thighs as she clenched around him over and over again. She couldn't even open her eyes the pleasure and exhaustion was so consuming.

Chad suddenly flipped them over so she was beneath him. He grabbed her leg, pulling it up high and started thrusting in and out of her. *Too much*, she wanted to cry as her orgasm intensified to the point her entire body felt on fire.

He pushed hard into her, reaching deeper than she thought possible, and the fireworks exploded again before her first orgasm even finished. She yelled out as her body shook with pleasure, every inch of her skin tingling.

"Please," she pled.

He seemed to know just what she needed and moved off her, his own breath coming out in pants. They lay side by side as their breathing slowed and their bodies finally quit quivering.   "I think I may have just lost a few years off my life," Chad said with a chuckle. Bree smiled, she knew how he felt.

"I can't open my eyes," she murmured, feeling better than anyone should be allowed to feel.

Chad pulled her close and she fell asleep within seconds.

When Bree woke again, Chad was next to the bed putting on pants. She sleepily got to her feet and put the discarded robe on. Her mind cleared quickly, and since her body was temporarily sated, her worries came back to the forefront.

She tilted her head and pointed toward the kitchen, then left the room, knowing he'd follow her. She'd get dressed later. She felt light headed and wanted nothing more than a hot cup of coffee. She'd even try eating a bagel or muffin. She knew her stomach needed something in it other than acid.

Bree walked to the coffee pot and started it brewing, then sat at the table. Chad entered the room behind her, grabbing a package from the cupboard and joining her at the table. He looked amazing in the morning with stubble dotting his chin, and low riding pajama bottoms. She didn't know what was wrong with her, but she wanted to crawl into his lap for round two and forget everything but the pleasure he brought her.

"Here, eat this," Chad told her as he placed a pastry in front of her. She pushed it back, the sugary donut turning her stomach. "You have to eat. You've already lost too much weight," he insisted as he pushed it back to her. She glared at him for a moment, but he didn't back down, so she finally took it.

Bree broke off a piece and placed it in her mouth, surprised by the burst of flavor on her tongue. Maybe she was hungry. After all, she'd had quite the intense workout a short time ago. She took another tentative bite, then polished off the donut in under a minute. Chad slid another one in front of her and she started picking at it, nibbling small bites. She missed the knowing grin on his face.

"Did you get any information last night? Who they were? What they wanted? Did the sheriff tell you anything?" Bree threw questions at Chad, no longer able to hold it in. She hoped he wouldn't treat her like a child. She needed to know.

She watched as he took a deep breath, like he was fighting with himself, before he finally let it out and looked her deep in the eyes. She felt almost giddy as she realized he was going to tell her something real – not try to protect her fragile feelings like her brothers kept doing.

As Bree waited, she had a small memory of racing down the road with her hand in the air. She'd been running away... She lost the thought and frowned in frustration.

"What is it?" Chad asked with concern.

"I remembered something, but..." she started to say, still concentrating.

"What did you remember?"

"Nothing huge, dang it. Just that my brothers are over-protective. I was trying to get away from them – trying to prove I could make it on my own. Is that how I ended up with you?"

"Kind of," he answered vaguely, which made her want to throw the rest of her donut at him.

"It's gone now, what were you going to say?"

"The sheriff came up empty last night. Whoever was out there was long gone by the time we got a proper search formed. They were smart. Are you sure you're up for the whole story, Bree? I think it would be better for you not to know," he hedged. She had to push down her temper. She didn't want kid gloves – she wanted the truth.

"I can handle it," she said through clenched teeth.

"Fine. You have a stalker. He's been after you for months. He's the reason you were in the hospital, and apparently he hasn't given up, as last night proves. We have no leads on who it is, or how he's getting his information. He shouldn't have had any way of knowing you were here last night, but he did," Chad said, short and to the point.

"M… maybe he followed us," Bree stuttered. She was trying to act like his words weren't affecting her, but it was a lot to take in. Someone wanted to kill her. Why?

"I guess it would help if I could remember my past," she finally said.

"Not really. We didn't know anything before you were shot. You racked your brain trying to figure out who it could be. We've done background checks on ex-boyfriends, old friends, people you've come in contact with. They've all had alibis for the times when events have taken place. We've come up with nothing but dead ends," he trailed off in frustration.

"Maybe he followed us from the hospital," she said, trying to keep the fear from her voice. She'd asked him to be honest with her; she didn't want him to regret that decision.

"I was watching for that, it's not possible."

Bree sat back and thought about it. She wished she could just wake up and everything would be right with her world. Had she led some kind of double life her family knew nothing about? Was she really a double agent with top secret information? For all she knew, she could be a horrible person who deserved to be hunted like an animal.

"It's not your fault. I can see the wheels turning in your head. Whoever this creep is, it's not about you, it's about him. You've done nothing to deserve this," Chad assured her. She didn't know if she believed him.

"I shouldn't stay here. It seems he's determined to get to me, and anyone who's in his way could get hurt," she said, trying to sound reasonable.

"Do you honestly believe I'd let you deal with this on your own. Even if you weren't carrying my child, I wouldn't let you leave my side. I will keep you safe."

"I don't know why, but it feels like we've had a discussion like this before," she said with a smile in her voice.

"My motto *is* to serve and protect."

"So, do we just hide out like victims, or can we have some kind of a life while we wait for the other shoe to drop?"

"I've never been one to hide. We'll up security, make sure guards are on duty twenty-four-seven, and we'll live somewhat normally. I don't want you going anywhere alone, though – not even to the backyard."

"I won't be treated like a child. I can agree to security, but you're being absurd," she retorted.

"I love it when you get all riled up," he said as he slowly stood.

Bree wasn't in the mood for games, but she could see he was.

"I'm still mad at you, Chad," she said, but she slowly rose from the table and took a step back.

"Doesn't bother me. You're mad at me a lot."

"Then maybe you should change the way you act," she said as she skirted the table. He slowly followed her, making her heart speed up.

"I haven't had too many complaints about the way I act, certainly not earlier this morning," he answered as he made a quick veer to the right. She dodged him and kept him at a safe distance – or so she thought.

"Maybe I just didn't want to hurt your feelings," she said, but couldn't keep the laughter from spilling out as he almost slipped on the smooth tile.

"You also moan a lot when you're underneath me," he said. She noticed his pants expanding. Their bantering was turning him on. It sent an arrow of desire straight through her. She didn't know how she could possibly want him again after being so fully satisfied.

"That's not very gentlemanly to say."

"I've never claimed to be a gentleman."

"Finally you say something that makes sense," she laughed. He lunged again, but she managed to avoid him. She knew he was toying with her. If he really wanted to catch her, she'd be on the ground in moments. Him allowing her to think she held some kind of power was exhilarating, though. She knew how she wanted their game to end.

Chad looked her in the eye and lifted his hand to the waistband of his flannel pants. Her breathing thickened as she waited. His body was sinful in its perfection. Her eyes stayed glued to his large fingers as they slipped under the elastic.

She practically drooled when they dropped to the floor and he stood before her with nothing on. She could feel the saliva building in her mouth. She wanted to taste him, run her tongue along his washboard abs, straight down to his manhood, and slip his head deep into her mouth.

She gave up on the game of chase and took a step toward him, her eyes finally lifting to his, which were narrowed in desire. The depths of his blue eyes were darkened to the color of a stormy ocean.

At that moment she held all the power – and yet none at all. He could bring her to her knees, but knowing she could do the same to him, made her able to stand.

Bree's trouble with stalkers, memory loss, and bullets flying all faded. She forgot about everything but the deep need inside her stomach – the burning sensation invading her body.

The phone rang.

"Ignore it," he commanded as he stepped toward her.

It rang over and over.

"Don't you have an answering machine?" she asked with frustration.

"Didn't think I needed one. I'm regretting that now," he said as it continued to ring. Their caller was persistent.

Chad finally stomped over to the phone and practically ripped it from the wall.

"This better be damn important," he yelled into the phone.

He paused as he listened, and Bree watched in frustration as he answered in one syllable clips. Within a minute, he was grabbing his pants and sliding them back on. She nearly screamed in sexual frustration.

Obviously the call was important. He'd quickly forgotten about their game.

"We'll be there," he finally said, then hung up the phone.

He turned to her and she knew she wasn't going to get her needs met. It was obvious from the anger on his face.

"That was your brother. There was a break in at your place last night. We're assuming it was after the bastard left here. This is the second time, now. We should've kept the place under surveillance, but we didn't think he'd go back," he said in frustration as he ran his fingers down his face. "I'm in your presence for thirty seconds and I seem to forget how to do my job," he sighed, almost as an afterthought.

"What do you mean *your job*?"

Chad looked at her like a dog that had just wet on the carpet.

"I repeat, what job are you referring to?"

"Don't get all bent out of shape. I just meant… I need to be watching out for you," he tried to cover.

"That's crap and you know it. Tell me the truth, now," she demanded.

"Okay, well, your brothers were worried about you, and rightfully so, because this creep was sending all kinds of letters about how you should be with him, so they figured you needed protection," he said.

"Are you my freaking bodyguard?" she demanded to know.

"It's not like that, Bree." He tried to pacify her.

"You are, aren't you?"

"Originally, yes, I was asked to guard you. But I'm not being paid to do it. I wanted to," he said in a half-truth. He hadn't wanted to babysit her in the beginning, but now they couldn't pay him to stay away.

"This just keeps getting better. So, what? You were guarding the princess, got bored, and decided to bed me to pass the time," she practically shouted.

"It wasn't like that. We slept together because neither of us could keep our hands off the other. You've never complained, so don't act all high and mighty," he shouted back.

Their morning wasn't going the way he wanted it to go, and he'd much rather be ripping her clothes off than fighting.

"We need to get ready and go to your place," he said as he walked to the bedroom. Bree was right behind him.

"I'm not going anywhere until you explain everything to me," she stormed.

Bree watched in amazement as he ignored her tantrum and walked into the bathroom, shutting the door with a resounding click. She thought about pounding on the wood until she drove him crazy, but finally decided to just get dressed. He wasn't going anywhere – she'd get information one way or the other.

Chapter Thirteen

Bree stepped into her home and looked around. She was hoping the familiar surroundings would jar her memory, but the more she looked over her items, the more frustrated she became. She didn't feel a personal connection to any of it. Nothing – not even when she saw the locket her mother had given her only months before her death.

"It's okay, Bree. You didn't live here very long. Don't expect a floodgate of memories to come flying back," Chad reassured her, reading the emotions on her face.

She watched as Chad joined her brothers and they looked through the apartment. Items were strewn across the floor and she looked in horror at her torn up clothing. Why would the person want to destroy her things? That didn't make any sense.

"Get out of my way. Where's my daughter? Why wasn't I called last night?" Bree heard the unmistakable voice of her father. She smiled, already feeling as if she knew him well.

"We didn't see a reason to alarm you. We had the situation under control," she heard Chad say, to which George started thundering again.

"Under control! My daughter was shot at, and you say the situation was under control. I ought to take you out back and whip you, boy," George roared. Bree figured it was a good time to get out there and save the men.

"Hi, Dad," she said as she walked up and gave him a hug.

His anger evaporated as he took her in his arms and held her so tightly she couldn't breathe. When she started gasping for air, he finally released his death grip.

"Are you okay, baby? I've been so worried. They should've called me," he said in a rush of words.

"I'm okay, Dad. They really did handle everything. It was late," she said, instantly regretting it when she saw the fire return to his eyes.

"I had to learn about the shooting from my friend who works at city hall. How do you think that makes me feel? My daughter is dodging bullets, and a virtual stranger is the one to tell me about it. I would think I'd raised you kids well enough that you'd call me in a crisis," he said, sounding more hurt than angry.

Bree quickly threw her arms back around him, and had to fight the tears wanting to escape. She couldn't stand hurting this man who'd been nothing but good to her.

"I'm sorry, I really am. Next time, we'll call you the minute something happens," she promised.

"I certainly hope there won't be a next time. I think you need to come back home," he said as if that would solve all problems.

Bree watched as Chad tensed on the other side of the room. She thought about taking the easy out and going home. She even tried to make herself nod her okay, but found herself shaking her head, instead. No matter how much she told herself to accept, her head wouldn't listen. She just kept shaking it, *no*.

She noticed Chad visibly relax at her refusal.

"I don't understand it. You're still as stubborn as ever, even with amnesia," he said, but there was also pride in his tone. She could see he was proud of her for taking a stance. For some reason, his approval meant a lot to her.

"I just want to keep you safe," he pled.

"I know you do. I'm overwhelmed with all the love you've given me. It would be a crime to lose an obviously great life," she said, soothing his feelings.

Though she was trying to make him feel better, she found that she meant the words. She wanted to remember her past, her family. Even if the worst were to occur and she never regained her past, she would love them anyway.

"Bree, maybe it would be better if you just went back home. I know you don't have your memory back, but as the only impartial person in the room, I think I can speak honestly without a lot of emotions getting involved. Someone is obviously out to get you, and you don't know who it is. It seems the smart thing to do would be to go home, where your family can keep you safe," Charlie said.

Bree looked at him blankly, not having a clue who he was.

"Sorry, Bree. This is Charlie, my best friend. You'll remember everyone after a while. He wanted to come to the hospital, but got called away on business," Trenton said.

"I'm Sorry, Charlie. I still don't have my memory back," Bree said, feeling bad when she saw the hurt expression on his face.

Bree looked over at Chad who was glaring daggers at Charlie and not even trying to hide it. It seemed Chad didn't like another good-looking man in the room who wasn't related to her. Bree's hackles stood up and she gave Charlie a hug, partly to make up for not knowing who he was, and partly to show Chad she could do whatever she liked. She could swear she heard him growl. She smiled.

"We may as well sit down and try to figure this out," George said, and Charlie released her. Bree thought that was wise, considering she noticed Chad took a menacing step toward them. She decided to back off Charlie before a fist fight started.

She sat on the couch, where Chad quickly joined her, cutting Charlie off. The testosterone was thick in the room. Bree wanted to get up and open a window, but dutifully stayed where she was.

"I may not have my memory back, but I know I want independence. I feel safe at Chad's ranch, and I don't think there's any need for me to be moved. I'm not a child, and I don't need to run home every time I get scared. I hope you can all understand that," Bree stated with little emotion in her voice. She wanted to make a point without hurting feelings.

"You know we're all just concerned about your safety. If you come home until the person after you has been caught, then none of us will complain when you want your independence," Trenton said.

"Do you run home each time you receive a threat?" Bree asked. Trenton laughed as if what she said was funny, until she raised her eyebrow, letting him know she was waiting for an answer.

"That's different, Bree," Trenton said.

"How so?"

"Well... um... you know," he hedged.

"No. Obviously, I don't know. So please explain it to me," she said, not backing down.

"It's just that, well, I'm a guy," he said, and her eyes fired at him. If looks could kill, Trenton would be dead where he sat.

"That is completely chauvinistic and you know it. Just because I'm a girl, doesn't mean I'm less than any of you. I've obviously managed to stay alive this long. I'll admit, getting shot and losing my memory is not the most fun experience I've had, not that I can remember those times right now, but still. You can't treat me like a five year old child. You're acting like pigs," she said as she looked into the eye of each man in the room.

They looked down uncomfortably, then Chad squeezed her hand. She turned on him.

"I may be choosing to stay with you, but the same goes for you. I'm only staying because I think it's important for me to know the father of my child. I won't be treated like an invalid," she said, causing the smile to drop from his lips.

"I don't..." he began.

"Yes, you do, and it needs to stop. I don't mind you wanting to protect me, but you won't keep information from me anymore, *and* you'll treat me as an equal. My son or daughter won't think their father is the all-mighty, while their mother is a weakling," she said. Chad grinned before leaning down and kissing her square on the mouth, taking the rest of her words away.

"Very well said," he agreed, but she could see the twinkle in his eyes. They'd talk more once they were in private.

"I'm proud of what a strong woman you've become, Bree. I won't ever stop worrying about you, but rest assured that I worry just as much about your insufferable brothers. I'm a father, and that's what we do. You'll soon understand how I feel," George said as he pointedly glanced at her stomach. He was visibly upset – but trying to hide it.

Bree hated knowing she'd upset her father, but she couldn't back down or she'd never regain the ground she'd managed to forge for herself. She had to stay firm – but that didn't mean she had to be cruel.

"You all trusted Chad enough to appoint him as my personal babysitter, so you should trust him enough to continue the job," Bree said, glaring at Trenton, who squirmed in his seat.

"You're pregnant?" Charlie asked in stunned disbelief, causing all eyes to turn to him.

"I can't believe I didn't tell you," Trenton said. "With everything else going on, I forgot. Sorry, man."

"And you're the father," Charlie practically spit at Chad. "Maybe if you were more concerned about her safety, instead of getting her into bed, she might not have been shot."

Chad's eyes widened at Charlie's words, and Bree felt him tense next to her. She knew he was about ready to jump up and pound the guy.

"Listen, you son of a…" Chad started to say.

"Come on guys. Let's not let this get out of hand," Trenton interrupted, standing up so he could play referee if things escalated.

"Are you seriously going to let this piece of work be alone with her?" Charlie practically yelled.

"Are you kidding me? I don't know you, but you're way out of line. I'd back down if I were you." Chad spoke with so much authority, Bree expected Charlie to back off, but the man was either an idiot or had a death wish.

"Bree, this guy's taking advantage of you. He obviously can't keep you safe. His focus has been on taking your innocence more than doing his job," Charlie said and made a move to take her hand.

Chad jumped between Charlie and Bree so quickly Trenton didn't have time to blink, let alone stop him. Chad slammed his fist into Charlie's chest, sending him flying back and then pinned him against the wall.

"I don't care if you are Trenton's best friend. If you try to touch her again, you won't walk for a month. Do I make myself clear?"

"Okay, this is ridiculous. Chad, let him go. He's just worried about Bree. He's known her since she was a toddler," Trenton said, tugging on Chad's immovable shoulder.

"Can we please leave now," Bree whispered, wanting them to leave before the situation got worse than it already was. Chad immediately responded to her and dropped Charlie as if he were nothing more than a sack of potatoes.

"I'm sorry," he said, sincerely regretting the loss of his temper.

"Bree, I'm sorry, I'm just so worried about you," Charlie called out as she headed to the front door.

She turned around and looked at the man, who was close to weeping. She felt bad for him. He must care about her a lot, and she had no clue who he was.

"I know, Charlie, but I need to get out of here," she said, then walked from the room with Chad's arm around her. Her father followed her out the door, but her brothers gave her space.

"Whether you get your memory back or not, my dear, you'll soon discover our family is passionate. Emotions always run high, but if someone we love is in danger, they shoot through the roof. Just know we love you and you can count on us for anything," George said, giving her a hug goodbye.

"I know, Dad. Being here isn't doing me any good, though. I'd rather just leave and let everyone cool off. I promise I'll call you later tonight, okay?" she said, hoping he'd understand.

"Okay. I'll feel better if you do," he answered.

"I will, I promise."

George let them walk away and Bree felt instantly calmer the moment she sat down in Chad's familiar truck. She didn't want to go back to the ranch, but she may have hyperventilated if she'd stayed in that place for one moment longer.

"How about we go to a movie?" Chad asked. She could kiss him, she was so happy with his suggestion. A calm movie was just what the doctor ordered.

"That sounds wonderful, but only if it's a romantic comedy," Bree replied. Chad groaned but navigated the truck toward the Cinemark complex. They studied the selections, and Bree nearly jumped up and down when she spotted, *The Lucky One by Nicholas Sparks*.

Chad groaned but he reluctantly purchased the tickets and took her to see the movie. He enjoyed watching it through her eyes. She cried, laughed, and snuggled in close to him. It was a nice break from the stress that seemed to always consume their lives.

"Thanks again, Chad. That was just what I needed," Bree said as they walked to his truck.

"There's nothing I won't do for you," he told her, realizing he meant the words. She could ask for the moon, and he'd do his best to get it for her. She looked in his eyes and something shifted.

Bree didn't know which of them moved first, but suddenly she was melting in his arms as his mouth gently caressed her lips. The moment stretched, filling her with a sense of rightness and love. He could be passionate and aggressive, or gentle and loving. He seemed to know what she needed exactly when she needed it.

His cell phone rang and Chad seriously considered throwing it against the building across the street. He didn't care who was calling, he wasn't getting interrupted again.

"Woo hoo, ride that cowboy," someone called out, and Chad groaned against her mouth. It looked like he couldn't catch a break.

He reluctantly pulled away, nearly changing his mind when he saw Bree's flushed cheeks and swollen lips. Her eyes slowly opened, full of confusion – probably wondering why he stopped. He was going to take her to a deserted island – no phones, no kids, no teenagers and no stalkers.

His phone went off again and he pulled the annoying device from his pocket. Bree just buried her head against his shoulder, seemingly as frustrated as him.

"What?" he snapped into his phone. After a pause, he spoke again.

"Is it necessary? She's been through a lot the last couple days."

"Fine," he answered, then hung up.

"The police have someone in custody. They think we should come in," Chad told her. Bree's eyes widened, but he was impressed by how quickly she squared her shoulders and pulled herself together.

"Then we'd better get down there," she said without hesitation.

"I can deal with it on my own," Chad offered.

"No. I want answers. I want this to be over," she answered and he heard the steel in her voice.

Chapter Fourteen

Bree's stomach turned as they stepped inside the huge double doors of the sheriff's station. She glanced at the reception area with people calling out orders, and chaos reigning. Somewhere among the throng of individuals could be the one responsible for disrupting her life, shooting her in the head, and endlessly pursuing her.

She squeezed Chad's hand tightly in her own. She was unaware he was scoping the room, looking for possible exits, noticing anyone looking suspicious.

This could be the end of the chase. She could possibly start focusing on her life and getting her problems worked out, without having to look over her shoulder every five minutes. If the person after her was caught, then she could focus on her child, and if she were relaxed, then maybe she'd get her memory back.

She smiled at the thought. She really wanted to know her past – her family.

Chad led her to the reception desk, where a harried looking woman in uniform barely glanced away from her computer screen as they approached.

"How can I help you?" she practically yelled, reaching into her messy hair and grabbing a pen that had seen better days.

"We're here to see Captain Musket," Chad replied. That seemed to snap her to attention.

"Name?"

"Chad Redington and Bree Anderson."

She typed something on her computer keyboard, dropping the pen on her desk.

"ID, please," she said while sticking her hand out, her eyes still glued to the monitor. Chad reached into his wallet at the same time as Bree pulled her purse forward. They handed over their ID's and waited while she typed something else.

"Head over to the door on the far right. Deputy Mitchel will let you through," she said without as much as a smile. Bree felt like a criminal for all the warmth the woman showed. She'd hate to be on the wrong side of the law.

"This way, please," Deputy Mitchel said when Bree took too long to move forward. She jumped at the sound, then followed Chad's assured steps as he made his way toward the huge officer. He looked around the room, his hand resting on his gun, before opening the door for them. "Go down this hallway, turn right. It's interrogation room number two. Wait there and the Captain will meet you."

Chad pulled Bree along as they made their way down the plain, narrow hallway. They passed a door where she heard someone shouting and a chill went down her spine. The place gave her the creeps.

Bree had always been curious what a jail was like from the inside. How the cells looked, if the interrogation rooms really were the same as they appeared on her favorite crime dramas. Now that she was there, her curiosity took a nose dive. She couldn't wait to get back out into the fresh air. She didn't understand how prisoners could stand the confined space, day in and day out. It was too much.

They stood where the officer told them to and waited.

"Are you okay?" Chad asked, startling Bree out of her thoughts.

"I was thinking I wouldn't want to be locked up in one of these places. Just standing here in the hallway is intimidating enough," she answered with a nervous laugh.

"This is luxurious, believe it or not. I've been places overseas that still give me nightmares," he said in a voice that made Bree realize she didn't want to hear further details of those experiences. If he wanted to talk, she'd listen, but she knew it would rip her apart. She knew nothing of his life, nothing at all about the father of her unborn baby.

"Sorry to keep you waiting, Chad, Bree," Captain Musket said as he stepped up to them with his hand out. He was a pleasant looking man, appearing to be in his sixties; probably about five feet seven, with a round belly. Even with his weight, he still looked like he'd be able to take down a criminal if the need arose. By the twinkle in his eye, Bree had a feeling he'd love for someone to get out of hand. She liked him instantly.

"We understand. You're a busy man," Chad replied.

"Let's step into the viewing room so Bree can look at who we have," the Captain said while opening a door. Bree was the first to enter, coming face to face with a dreadful looking man. She didn't have any clue who he was, but his cold gaze froze her, staring directly at her through the window.

"Don't worry, Bree. He can't see you. He just knows we can see him and he's trying to intimidate you. This room is soundproof so he doesn't even know we're in here for sure. He's just assuming," the Captain assured her.

She watched as the man placed his hands on the window and leaned his head forward. He stuck his tongue out and swiped it up the glass. His greasy black hair looked like it hadn't been washed in a month, and the scar on his cheek proved he'd been in at least one fight. But nothing compared to the dead look in his eyes. Bree jumped back, completely disgusted.

Chad bunched his fist, having to fight the urge to punch the bullet proof glass, rattling the window, to surprise the creep.

"He's a winner," the Captain said with a disgusted sigh. "Is anything coming to you, Bree?"

"No, I don't have any idea who he is or what he could possibly want."

"Do you want to stay in here and watch the interview?"

"No, he said he wanted to speak to me, so I'll go in there. I refuse to let him intimidate me," she said with resolve. The Captain patted her back, then opened the door and waited. Bree took a deep breath before she stepped out. She could do this. She wouldn't let any person control her emotions, especially a disturbing, pathetic man.

"Hey, sexy lady. You can use my lap if you want a more comfortable seat," the man said with a leer as Bree entered. She heard Chad curse behind her, and she put out her hand to touch him, letting him know she was fine.

"I'm fine in a chair. What do you want?"

"Is that any way to act when a man calls on you?"

"You can cut the act, or sit it off in a cell. Your choice," Captain Musket said, bending down on the table and pressing his face up close to the man's.

"You're just no fun, are you?" he sneered, but he leaned back, intimidated by the Captain.

"Not with dirt bags like you."

"What the hell do you want? Spit it out," Chad said as he took a seat facing the man. Bree slowly sat next to Chad, her leg brushing against his, keeping her grounded, reassurance that he was right there.

"Look, I've been trying to get an honest job in this town for a year, but because of my past record, no one wants to give me a chance. So this guy approaches me and asks if I want to make some money. Of course I wanted to make money, not like anyone is handing out jobs," the man started speaking.

"What man?" Chad interrupted.

"He's not the type of guy who gives you a name, you know? I just called him Mr. X. Well, I was just supposed to write these letters and stuff. Trail a girl. Nothing big – not anything that could get me in any real trouble, and he was paying well – real well," the man continued.

"You consider scaring an innocent woman not a crime?" Chad demanded.

"I didn't break the law. It wasn't like I tried to touch her or anything," the man defended himself.

Chad stood up from the table, leaned down and got in the man's face. The guy scooted his chair back, fear displayed in his eyes.

"Okay, you're a freaking boy scout. Do you have any useful information for us?" The Captain interrupted before things got out of hand.

"Well, things started escalating. Mr. X wanted me to break into her house and take some items. I wasn't going down for that crap. I know the lock-up time for breaking and entering. I was just supposed to shadow her, you know? I'm not up for the hard core stuff. I've cleaned up my act – learned my lesson," he said with a fake smile.

Bree knew the man was full of it. She wouldn't put it past him to do anything for a few bucks.

"Besides, I didn't get paid after the last time I hand delivered a note. I'm out there risking my reputation, and he stiffs me," the man stated.

Bree realized why he was so willing to turn over his boss. He wasn't getting money any longer, so he had nothing to lose. He thought maybe he could get out of charges if he came forward instead of being busted.

"How did you get ahold of this man?" the Captain asked.

"He gets ahold of me. I don't have contact information on him. But, I thought you could do one of those wire thingy deals, or something like that. I'd be willing to risk my life… if there were some benefit to me," he smirked.

"Do you seriously think we're going to pay you after what you've done? You're going to be lucky to get out of jail in the next five years," the Captain thundered. He was obviously furious at what was looking more and more like a waste of all their time.

"Look, I didn't have to come forward," the man said, starting to sweat as he squirmed around in his chair.

"You came forward because you thought it could somehow benefit you, you piece of crap," Chad said. He was sick of speaking to the low-life thug, and he didn't think they were going to get anything useful out of him.

"Wait!" he shouted when it was obvious he'd lost their attention. "I know he's going to be calling me soon. He said he has something real big planned for the upcoming holiday," the man said, trying to hook the bait.

"I'm not listening to this anymore. You're obviously where you belong," Bree said. She couldn't stand the stench of the man any longer and wanted out of the room. She felt like the walls were starting to close in around her.

"You high and might b…" he started to say, when Chad reached out and backhanded him across the room.

"I dare you to complete that sentence," Chad said, itching to pummel him.

The man glared at him, then turned his head and spat a stream of blood.

"That's assault. I want to press charges," he shouted to the Captain, who was looking at the door.

"What? I didn't see anything. It looks to me like you tripped over the legs of the table. You really should work on your balance," the Captain said with a serious face.

"All you high and mighty pieces of crap stick together. I'll sue you – all of you. I know you have lots of money, little girl. Mr. X talked all about what a rich family you come from. I'll own everything you have. This is brutality," he shouted.

Bree had to fight the sudden urge to laugh. The man was pathetic and he couldn't help them. Her hopes had been raised for nothing. She stepped past him, and at the last minute dug her three inch heel into his shoeless foot. He screamed out, but Bree was at the door before he made a lunge for her.

Chad threw his elbow back, connecting with the man's head, sending him sprawling to the floor. His yelling stopped as he was knocked unconscious.

"Let's go," Chad told her. Neither of them looked back as the Captain ordered one of his deputies to lock the man up.

"Have you verified his name? Done a background check?" Chad asked as they made their way down the hall.

"Got his name. Robert Loren. Just a small-time petty thief. He served about five years up state and has been out for two. He hasn't held a job longer than two weeks, but I don't think he's capable of being the mastermind behind this. I think he's telling the truth," the Captain stated.

"I agree. I was hoping he had useful information when you called, though."

"Me too, I'm sorry to have wasted your time," the Captain said.

"I'm glad we came, and we did get some information. Apparently, Mr. X isn't finished with his games," Bree said. She was more furious than afraid at that moment.

"Go home. If I get any other information, I'll call right away," the Captain said while leading them back to the lobby.

"It's been a rough day. We'll start over tomorrow," Chad told her as he led her down the stairs and over to his truck.

He helped her inside, then walked around and started the vehicle. They were silent on the way home, both lost in their own thoughts.

Chapter Fifteen

Bree woke up to a beautiful, bright, sunny morning and decided she needed a walk. She knew Chad would be furious, but it had been several weeks since anyone had shot at her, left ominous notes, or tried to kidnap her. The ranch was surrounded by security men and she was safe to walk the short distance to the lake. She'd deal with Chad's lecture – it was worth it to get a little alone time.

She quickly showered and dressed in a light summer dress, thankful for a rare day of warmth in the unpredictable Washington weather. She didn't bother with makeup or doing her hair, just threw it up in a messy bun and called herself good.

Her foul mood the last few days had chased Chad to the barn, and even caused her brothers to back off. She was tired of being treated like the princess Chad had called her. She was a woman, and it was time he knew it.

Chad hadn't so much as kissed her since their last encounter, which had been cut short by the call from the police, and she thought she may die of sexual frustration. She didn't want to be the one to make the first move – that was his job. His idea that them being intimate clouded his ability to protect her was getting on her nerves.

Maybe if she agreed to marry Chad, he'd actually take her to bed again.

Bree reached the pond and sat down, grabbing a handful of rocks and tossing them in the water, one by one, watching the ripples as they floated further from her.

She leaned her head back and enjoyed the sounds around her. She could hear noises from the cows in the pasture, the horses neighing, and all kinds of woodland creatures playing in the nearby woods. It was peaceful, relaxing, and soon she found herself drifting to sleep.

Bree stirred restlessly on the ground, her nightmare causing her body to sweat and her muscles to tense. Chad was standing such a short distance away. He was yelling something at her, but she couldn't hear him. She could see his mouth moving, but no sound was coming out.

Then, there was a man wearing a dark mask. He had a gun and it was pointed right at Chad. *No!* she screamed, but Chad wouldn't face the man. All of a sudden a shot rang out and she watched as he collapsed to the ground.

Bree jerked awake, tears falling down her face. She turned her head, trying to get her bearings. Where was she? Where was Chad? He was hurt – she had to help.

Upon becoming fully awake, she realized she'd only been dreaming, and vivid details of her nightmare came flooding back to her, overwhelming her in their intensity. Suddenly the fog in her mind began to lift and color filled its place, bringing her lost memories to life.

She remembered everything. Chad getting shot, the men capturing her, Chad saving her, and the man facing them, firing his gun. She flinched, remembering the fear as she saw that small puff of smoke rising from his gun right before the bullet struck.

Bree sat by the water for another half hour, too shaken up to move. With her memories back, she couldn't stop the overwhelming emotions that followed.

After compiling all the pieces of the last several months together, she felt such relief at the picture of her life she was able to visualize again. She was one-hundred-percent in love with Chad. She'd started falling in love with him before she was hurt, but was even more in love now. He'd been by her side night and day – risked his own life for her. She couldn't imagine being without him.

Her hand moved down to her still flat stomach as she fully comprehended she was having his child. They'd made a baby together. Their child was strong like its father. Her pregnancy survived Bree being shot, sitting in the hospital in a coma, and all the stress known to cause miscarriages.

Bree was filled with unbelievable joy at how her life had changed so much in only a few short months.

She had to find Chad. His quest of keeping them platonic was about to end because if he didn't take her to bed soon, he may see a true tantrum from the princess. She laughed aloud at her own joke.

Ah, she missed Jennifer, her brother's wife. They'd become so close since she'd married Trenton. Bree hurt thinking about how hard this must have been on her best friend. Jennifer hadn't shown how hurt she must have felt at Bree's forgotten memories of their bond, but Bree knew if the situation was reversed, she'd be devastated.

She had to call her.

Well, after she spent alone time with Chad.

"Bree," she heard Chad shout. She grinned in anticipation. His tone sounded furious, mixed with a twinge of worry. She'd broken his rule of never going anywhere alone. *Bring it on*, she thought. Their fights always ended most satisfyingly.

"Over here," she called, then heard his footsteps racing toward her. She grinned more. She knew he could move silently through the woods. He wanted her to know he was coming. Her stomach tightened with raw need.

Chad came to a halt five feet in front of her. He quickly scanned the area before turning back to glare at her. She smiled sweetly at him. She wasn't ready to tell him her memory was back. He'd played with her, now it was her turn to play with him.

"You aren't supposed to go off by yourself," he finally said between clenched teeth.

"I needed a walk," she answered sweetly.

She watched as his forehead wrinkled. She could practically hear him counting in his head. Oh, how she loved pushing his buttons.

"It's for your own safety," he finally muttered.

"As you can see, I'm alive and well," she answered in the same tone she knew was grating on his nerves. Her nipples grew hard, and she felt heat building. She tried to tell herself anticipation was half the fun, but she was about out of patience. She was salivating at the thought of his thick erection plunging into her. She looked down his body and licked her lips when she saw him tense at her overly sexual glance.

"What are you… what's going on?" he stammered.

"I'm hungry, Chad, famished in fact." She looked at his painted on jeans, open shirt, and sexy cowboy hat and she felt like flames were igniting all over her. Her skin burned and her core pulsed. She was about to go off without a single touch from him. He was all man – and he was hers.

She saw him shift, watched his jeans tighten as he became aware of her arousal. He shifted as he tried to maintain his anger, but she saw his eyes dilate. She knew she'd won. Bree reached up and undid the top button on her dress. Then she slowly moved down and released the next one.

She felt triumphant as his eyes practically jumped from their sockets as she moved down her dress, exposing her tempting cleavage.

"Bree," he groaned. He didn't move, just watched as she performed her strip tease.

"Yes," she panted as her dress fell open, exposing her lacy green bra. Her nipples were beaded into hard buds and poking uncomfortably against the fabric, but even that was erotic.

She slipped her hands into the waistline of her dress and with a quick shimmy, it floated to the ground, leaving her standing before him in nothing but her lacy bra and matching panties, which barely covered her womanhood from his view.

Chad finally moved forward and pressed her body against him. His hungry kiss left her even more breathless and she reached up and grabbed ahold of his hair, holding on for dear life.

"We should go inside," he gasped as he pulled back a fraction of an inch.

"Now," she demanded, not wanting to take the time to go anywhere. The sun felt amazing on her nearly naked body, his arms were around her, and she felt free from the prison she'd been locked in for months. She leaned forward and bit his bottom lip, eliciting another groan from him.

He gripped her butt and pulled upward, grinding her wet womanhood into the rough fabric of his jeans. She wrapped her legs around his waist and moved her hips, sliding against him, so close to completion with barely a touch.

Chad deepened the kiss, his tongue slowly moving in and out of her mouth, mimicking the love making she so deeply desired. She wanted him inside her, filling her. Seductively grinding against him again, he seemed to take the hint. He moved them backward to a huge boulder next to the edge of the woods.

The spot offered a semblance of privacy, not that either of them noticed, but better yet, offered them a place to sit. She pushed down on him as her feet touched the rock, giving her leverage to better move.

"What you do to me," he groaned as her breasts pushed against him. Ripping off his open shirt, he then dispersed with her bra and cupped her heavy breasts. She leaned back, giving him better access and he bent his head and took her nipple in his mouth, alternating biting down and sliding his tongue across the pebbled pink bud.

He squeezed them together, moving his head back and forth, driving her insane as he pleasured her nipples over and over.

She reached her hands down and unclasped the buttons on his jeans, pushing her hand inside the tight denim until she hit payday and wrapped her fingers around his silky smooth erection. She pulled it free, rubbing her thumb across the head, nearly giddy when moisture dripped out, showing her how ready he was for her.

Chad cried out when she ran her nail across the sensitive tip, then down his long length. Then she gripped him tightly and moved her fist up and down several times.

With another groan, Chad released her breasts and ripped off her panties, leaving her naked on his lap. He closed his mouth on hers at the same time that he thrust hard inside her hot, wet core.

"Oh… I've missed you, Chad," she cried out, the intense feeling of pleasure causing so many emotions to rush through her newly found mind. She didn't want gentle. She didn't want slow. She wanted fast and hard, and now!

She ground herself against him, her swollen nub rubbing against the base of his erection, making her cry out. He gripped her hips tightly in his and pushed up in her.

Bree gripped his shoulders and used the rock as leverage as she met him thrust for thrust. Her thigh muscles burned as the two of them moved together, but she ignored it. She ignored everything but the immense sensations washing through her.

"Yes…" she called as her body convulsed with release. She gripped him tightly as wave after wave of pleasure washed through her. Then he cried out as he pushed so hard against her, she didn't know where he ended and she began and she continued to ride the wave with him.

Bree was spent. She couldn't move a single muscle if she had to. She laid her head on Chad's shoulder and soaked up the sun on her back and the feel of his hands caressing her damp skin. She took in the moment – the intensity – the love.

Chad didn't move for several minutes. Eventually he placed his hand under her chin and lifted her face so she had no choice but to look at him. She gave him a sheepish grin.

"What the hell was that?" he asked.

"I wanted you."

"I always want you," he replied with his own smile. It seemed their fight was over. "I usually have more restraint than to ravage you in the open, though."

"I'm glad you didn't resist," she said, then leaned in and sucked his bottom lip into her mouth. Chad grabbed her hips and moved her off him so suddenly her legs almost gave out. She caught herself at the last second.

"Not a chance. We need to get you dressed before one of my hands come wandering out here," he commanded as he turned around. She walked up and wrapped her arms around his back, trailing her fingers down his stomach.

"Are you sure?"

"You're trying to kill me, aren't you?" he said with a chuckle. He turned and gave her a quick kiss on the nose, before bending to retrieve her dress. He slipped it over her head before he realized her bra was still on the ground.

He shook his head, then picked up the green lace and stuffed it in his pocket. Bree gave up and started buttoning her dress. He'd satisfied her initial itch; she could wait ten minutes to get to his bedroom before starting round two.

"If this causes death, then yes, I am. Meet me in the bedroom and I'll…" she whispered the rest in his ear and felt extreme pride when she watched his chest compress as the air left his body, and he gaped at her. She turned and ran toward the house.

She heard him quickly catching up behind her. Just as she ran through the kitchen door, the phone went off.

"It can wait," he said as he pinned her to the wall.

"You know it might be important," she countered. She wanted to ignore it but he still didn't have a stupid answering machine.

"Why does this damn phone ring at the worst possible moments," was Chad's greeting. She giggled as she ran her hands along the bulge in his jeans.

"When?" The tone of his voice stopped Bree. Something was wrong.

"We'll be there," he said before hanging up. He turned and the look in his eye made Bree want to run. She didn't want to know what he had to say.

"Bree..." he began.

"No, I don't want to know," she said, holding up her hand.

"Honey, I'm sorry. It's your dad. He's had a heart attack."

It was too much to comprehend on top of all she had endured. She couldn't lose her dad, not now when she needed him the most. In her body's final attempt at survival mode, Bree fainted, barely giving Chad time to catch her before she hit the kitchen floor.

Chapter Sixteen

"What?" Bree asked as she came to. Chad was pressing a cold compress to her face. "What's going on?"

"We have to go. Your father had a heart attack. I don't know how bad it is, they just said to get down there right away," Chad answered. The worry in his eyes made her stomach clench. She just got her memory back, plus her dad was too young, so full of life. Their family couldn't survive the loss. Losing their mother was hard enough.

"I'm sorry, let's go," she told him as she got to her feet. Her knees were shaking but she was determined to stay strong.

Chad placed his arm around her as he led her to his truck. They were silent on the way to the hospital, stress keeping them from speaking. Bree hadn't told Chad she got her memory back, but that could wait.

Chad made the normally thirty minute drive in half the time, but it still felt like it took forever. Bree was jumping from the truck before he had it in park. He quickly caught up to her as she rushed through the emergency room doors.

"George Anderson, please," Bree demanded.

"One moment please," the nurse replied as she typed on her keyboard. Bree drummed her fingernails on the counter, staring a hole through the nurse's head. After taking much longer than Bree thought necessary, the nurse finally looked up.

"He's being attended to by the doctor, now. If you have a seat in the waiting room, someone will notify you of his progress as soon as we know something," the woman said, then looked back down at her computer.

"That's it? You can't give me any other information. How would you like it if it was your father back there? Would you just want to sit quietly and wait?" Bree yelled at the cold woman.

"I'm sorry, Ma'am, but there's no other information we have at the moment. The doctors are doing all they can," the woman answered calmly. She was more than used to worried family members yelling at her.

"Bree," Joseph called as he rushed through the doors.

Bree turned and ran to her uncle. He grabbed her up in a bear hug and she sobbed into his chest.

"It will be okay, Sweetie. Your father is a strong man. A heart attack won't keep him down," Joseph said. He was trying to reassure her but she heard the worry in his tone. He was afraid for his brother.

"They won't tell me anything," she sobbed.

"He just got here about ten minutes ago. Your brother called you from the chopper. We were all at the house, having a drink and visiting, when his face got real pale and he clutched his chest. I know the signs. I've seen a man have a heart attack before. We got him here fast, Bree. They say the first thirty minutes are the most important. Let's sit down and wait for the good doctor," Joseph said, speaking far more quietly than normal. His tone scared her worse than the not knowing. Her Uncle Joseph was supposed to be loud – not sober.

Soon, their entire family was in the waiting room, quietly talking, glancing at the clock, stress clearly visible on their faces. None of them liked the sterile room; all of them prayed George would be okay.

They'd all spent months in the hospital when their mother was dying. It had been heartbreaking watching her slowly wither away. Bree couldn't stand the quiet any longer. She jumped up and began pacing the room. Chad kept a close eye on her.

"Trenton Anderson?" the desk nurse called out. Everyone stood and turned at once, causing her professionalism to slip a tad before she quickly recovered.

"I'm Trenton," he said as he walked over.

"The doctor's on his way out," she said, making Bree want to hit her. They all turned toward the E.R. doors and waited.

Soon, the door opened and a man walked out, looking down at a chart in his hand. The room was completely silent. He finally looked up and Trenton stepped forward.

"Are you Trenton Anderson?"

"Yes."

"I'm Doctor Michaels. Would you like to follow me so we can speak in private?"

"No, this is all family and whatever you have to say, they're going to need to hear," he said, staying planted to the spot.

"That's your choice, Mr. Anderson. We have you listed as emergency contact, so I'll give you the information and you can relay it. Your father had a mild heart attack known as a Posterior Infarct, also known as Inferior Infarct. There was clogging in one of the branches of his right coronary artery. We were able to help him in time, and his condition is stable right now," the doctor said.

Bree's head whipped between her brother and the doctor, not understanding what they were talking about. Posterior Infarct? Inferior Infarct? What the heck? She just needed to see her father, physically see that he was okay.

"What does this mean?" Trenton asked.

"We need to run more test, he may need surgery, but his vitals are steady right now, which is encouraging. He's in the E.R. so he can only have two visitors at a time, and you need to stay calm and supportive. We don't want to raise his blood pressure, and if he thinks you're stressed, it can cause him stress as well."

"I understand. Can I see him now?"

"Yes, you can bring one person along."

"Please, Trenton?" Bree asked. He looked at her and held his hand out. She grabbed hold of him and followed the doctor through the double doors.

They made their way down a long white hallway and Bree looked only forward. She could hear weeping from one of the rooms and had to fight the tears choking her throat. She hoped to not have to step foot in another hospital for many years. She knew they saved lives, but being there was draining for her soul.

"Through here. Stay only ten minutes," the doctor said as he pointed to a closed door. Trenton didn't hesitate as he quietly pulled the door open.

Bree rapidly blinked her eyes as she saw her larger-than-life father lying in the small hospital bed with wires hanging from his arms. He was so pale, except for his bright red cheeks.

"Dad?" she whispered. If he was sleeping, she didn't want to wake him, but she really needed to hear the sound of his voice.

"Bree, come here, sweetheart," he croaked, and she rushed to his bedside and sank into the chair, quickly gripping the hand he held out to her.

"I remember, Dad," she said, needing to tell him. His eyes widened and brightened beneath the bright hospital lights.

"Ah, Baby, that's so wonderful. I knew it was only a matter of time." He knew exactly what she was talking about – of course he did, he was her Dad. She sniffled as she gave him a watery smile.

"I promise you, I'm going to be okay. There's no way I'm going to leave you kids. Besides, I have a brand new grandchild coming into this world who's going to need a lot of spoiling," he said with a gentle smile.

"I love you so much, Dad. Don't you ever scare me like this again," Bree demanded.

"I'll try not to, Princess," he answered, reverting to what he'd called her when she was just a young girl.

"You gave us all quite a scare, Dad," Trenton said as he took the seat on the opposite side of the bed.

"Ah, boy, you know your old man's too tough to let some clogged arteries keep him down. Stinking doctor is trying to blame food and liquor, but give me a week and I'll be dancing circles around that young punk," George said.

"I'm coming home and I'll make sure you stay on any diet the doctor puts you on. You're not invincible," Bree gently scolded him.

"I'd love to have you home, Bree, but I'm the parent here," he tried to sound commanding but couldn't quite pull it off while lying in a small bed hooked up to machines. Bree arched her eyebrows at him.

"We'll discuss it later," Bree promised. She didn't want to cause him stress right then.

"As much as I want you home, Bree, what will Chad think about that?" George asked.

Bree looked at him for a moment without having an answer. She was confused. She'd only just gotten her memory back and needed to really analyze what had happened since she'd met him. They had moved so quickly in their relationship, constantly under extreme circumstances.

"I honestly don't know, Dad," she answered. Even though he was hurt, he was still her father, and he always seemed to have the answers.

"Do you love him?" he asked her.

"Yes," she replied as she leaned in and gave him a soft kiss on the cheek. There was no point in lying to him.

"Mr. and Mrs. Anderson, your time is up," a nurse interrupted as she looked in the door.

"Come on, Betsy, they just got here," George grumbled.

"Don't you dare sass me, George," she said and it was obvious the two knew each other well. "Two more minutes," she compromised before looking pointedly at the clock, then them. She quietly closed the door and Bree had a feeling she was waiting on the outside of it, looking at her watch.

"We better go, Dad. You know the rest of the gang is anxious to get back here. If I'm not mistaken, Esther seemed pretty worried as she paced up and down the hallway," Trenton said with a twinkle in his eye.

"Don't you be starting any rumors," George said, but Bree noticed a bit more color infuse his cheeks. It looked to her like her father and Esther may have a little romance going on.

"I wouldn't think of it," Trenton replied. He stood up and kissed George's cheek before walking to the door and waiting for Bree to say Goodbye.

"I love you, Dad," she said as she bent down and clung to him, taking in a deep breath of his special dad scent.

"I love you more than you could ever imagine. Now, promise me you aren't going to worry about me. You need to be focused on my grandbaby."

"I can't promise not to worry just a little bit, but I do promise to take good care of this baby," Bree said.

"I can settle for that," George said with a small smile. "Now send in the troops."

The nurse popped back in and looked at them.

"We're leaving," Trenton grumbled. She was quite the rule enforcer.

"I'll meet you in the lobby. I need to use the bathroom," Bree told him. He seemed about to stop her, so she rubbed her stomach as a reminder.

"Okay, but don't take too long. I'm sure Chad's already pacing the lobby while waiting for you to get back," Trenton said. She realized her brother finally had respect for Chad. That was a good thing if there was any chance of him being her husband.

She turned down the hall and slipped in the bathroom, where she leaned against the door and took a deep breath. She allowed the tears to fall while she sank to the floor. It hadn't been easy for her to see the strongest man she knew looking so frail.

She finally got up, washed her face and deemed herself ready to emerge. When she stepped from the bathroom, her body took her left instead of right, though. She didn't want to head back to the lobby just yet. She needed a few more minutes before she faced the mob.

Bree turned a few corners and found herself lost. She knew that wasn't good. Chad wasn't going to be happy with her when she didn't return right away. Well, he'd have to get over it. They were in a public hospital where nothing could happen to her. There were security cameras and policemen all over the place.

She found an exit sign and stepped through the door, taking a deep breath of fresh air. It was much better smelling than the antiseptic smell of the hospital. She stepped further out and looked around, trying to figure out where she was. It looked like she was on the backside of the building. She started walking along the covered breezeway, figuring she had a ways to go before she made it back to the E.R. entrance.

"Bree," someone called. She tensed as she looked around. She was being ridiculous. There was no way any harm could come to her in a public place. There were people all around her.

"Bree," the voice called again and she turned, sighing in relief when she saw Charlie running up to her.

"You scared me, Charlie," she said with a relieved chuckle.

"Sorry about that. Everyone is looking for you. It seems you made the great escape," Charlie said with the same grin she remembered from their childhood.

"I didn't mean to. I just wanted a few minutes to myself before having to sit in the crowded waiting room again," she explained.

"I understand. It's still pretty intense in there. Do you want to walk down by the pond? I'll send Trenton a text and let him know where we are so they stop worrying," he offered. She knew she shouldn't. Chad was going to be having a cow. But then she tensed her shoulders and decided she'd like that very much.

Chad was going to have to get used to her having a mind of her own. They were on hospital grounds and she wasn't alone, she was with a family friend.

"That sounds perfect, Charlie. Make sure you let Trenton know, though, so the lecture isn't too bad when we get back," she said. Charlie took out his phone and typed in a message, before placing it back in his pocket.

Charlie stuck out his arm and Bree placed her hand through it and followed him along a flower strewn path. She could hear birds chirping and smiled in delight when a squirrel ran right in front of them and scaled a tree. It turned and made noises at them as if they were disturbing his home.

Bree laughed aloud at the expression on his face.

"I learned this hospital inside and out when my dad was here last year," Charlie said as they moved further away from the hospital. The closer they came to the pond, the more peaceful Bree felt. She hadn't realized how much stress the building placed on her.

"I heard about that, Charlie. I'm so sorry you lost him," Bree responded. So many unnecessary deaths. His father had only been fifty when a truck driver had slammed into his small car, putting him in critical condition. He'd hung on for three months before his body finally gave out.

"It was a hard time," Charlie said quietly. She squeezed his arm, offering her support.

They continued in silence until they reached a small stream that fed into a nice pond. There was a family of ducks swimming in it, and a couple benches on the side. No one else was around, which Bree was grateful for. She didn't want to make small talk with strangers.

"I can't believe you're pregnant," Charlie murmured.

"I know, me either," Bree replied, rubbing her hand across her flat stomach. If she had a bump, it would all seem more real.

"You know, I'd do anything for you, don't you," Charlie said as he turned and pulled her close to him. Bree started to feel a bit uncomfortable with the intimate gesture. She had to remind herself it was Charlie, Trenton's best friend for more years than she could remember.

"I know, Charlie. You're like a brother to me," she answered as she tugged against him, trying to subtly let him know she wanted him to let go. Instead of responding to her signals, he pulled her tight against his body, and she felt her stomach turn when she felt his erection pressing against her.

"I could be so much more than that, Bree," he said as he quickly bent his head and covered her lips with his.

***

"How is dad?" Austin asked as Trenton stepped through the doors.

Chad looked behind him, but the doors shut without Bree following. He stepped forward, wanting to know where she was. He waited for a minute before approaching Trenton.

"Is Bree staying with your Dad?"

"No, she's right behind me. She had to use the bathroom. I think she just needed a minute to herself. I wanted to get back out here so the next two could see Dad," Trenton answered.

"That would be me and Esther," Joseph said, not giving anyone else a choice. He took Esther's arm in his and they made their way through the double doors.

"I think we may be having another wedding here pretty soon," Trenton said as he watched the two of them disappear.

"You may be right," Lucas said with a smile. "You didn't say how your dad was."

"I don't like seeing him hooked up to those monitors, and he looks too pale, but he's a fighter. I know he's going to pull through."

"That's what we needed to hear," Lucas said as he patted Trenton's back.

Chad continued to watch the door. He was getting a bad feeling in his gut, and if Bree didn't get out there soon, he was hunting her down.

As he watched the clock, deciding she had five more minutes, the doors opened and Joseph stepped out with Esther at his side. She looked teary eyed, but not as concerned as she'd looked before going in.

Chad waited for Bree to come with them. The doors once again closed with no sign of her.

"Did you see Bree?" Chad asked.

Everyone turned, alerted by his tone.

"No, she wasn't in the hallway," Joseph said, his forehead creasing with worry.

"We need to do a search," Chad commanded, his body on instant alert. No one argued with him. The stalker still hadn't been caught, and they weren't taking chances.

"We'll go through the E.R." Mark said.

"I'll alert security and see if they can spot her on the cameras," Lucas said as he walked to the front desk.

"The rest of you span out. Check all the doors and the parking lot. You all have my number if you find her," Chad said as he rushed out the front doors. He tried not to panic. She most likely had just stepped outside for fresh air. He knew she couldn't stand the smell of the hospital. He tried calling her, but in their haste to get to the hospital, she'd left her phone at the ranch.

Chad tried reassuring himself that even if she had gone outside, there was no way for the stalker to know she was there, or be able to kidnap her with security everywhere. If he could shake the bad feeling, he'd feel a whole lot better.

Chapter Seventeen

Bree fought against Charlie as he defiled her lips, trying to access her mouth. She tried to tell him *no*, and that gave him the opening he was looking for. His tongue snaked out and slipped inside her mouth.

She gagged as he assaulted her. What had gotten into him? His hand crept down her back and gripped her backside, tugging her hard against his body, as he thrust his hips forward, forcing his arousal against her.

"Stop!" she yelled when he released her mouth. She grabbed at his hair, pulling his head so he'd get the clue she didn't want him kissing her.

"What are you doing?" she demanded.

"I love you, Bree. I always have and always will," he said as if it were obvious. "I've waited so long for you to be ready for a relationship, and then you get knocked up by that complete piece of crap. I can be your husband and raise your child. He isn't deserving of you. He doesn't know you like I do," Charlie said in an impassioned speech.

"Charlie, I'm sorry, but this isn't what I want," she told him.

His eyes darkened in rage and he reached his hand up and slapped her hard across the face. Bree felt fear spike through her as she fought to stay conscious. Who was this man she thought she knew?

"Do you think you're too good for me just because I don't have as much money as your family? I've always been there for you, Bree. We just need to get you away from here. I figured if things started happening and you got scared, you'd need me. I could be your savior, rescue you from the crazy stalker," he said. His eyes were wide as he spoke. Bree realized he wasn't exactly stable at that moment.

"Charlie, you're right, we really need to sit down and talk. I haven't been very good to you lately – too self-absorbed," she said, willing to do anything to get them back in sight of other people. She never should've walked off with him.

His shoulders relaxed at her words, but she knew she wasn't out of danger yet.

"I'm really worried about my father right now, Charlie. Can we stop by and see him, then we can leave and talk about us?" Bree asked in what she hoped was a convincing voice.

"No, we can't go back in there. If we do, Chad won't let you leave. Can't you see how obsessed with you he is?" Charlie asked as he shook her, making sure she was listening to him.

Bree thought that was rich, him calling Chad possessive, when he'd been stalking her, breaking into her home, and was holding her against her will at that very moment.

"I know, Charlie. He doesn't give me time alone, but we can sneak in the back door, and I can peak in on my father. I don't even have to go in the room with him," she pled. If she could just get inside the hospital, she could notify security and get away from the psychotic man.

She saw him considering her request, so with her stomach turning at the thought of touching him, she reached her hand up and cupped his cheek, trying to act reassuring that she actually cared about him.

He bent down and kissed her again, and she forced her body not to tense. She was so close to him taking her back. He pulled her tightly against him once more and she fought the tears wanting to fall. If he saw even an inkling of her disgust, he'd never let her in public again.

He pulled away and looked in her eyes, then his narrowed.

"You almost had me fooled. You're just trying to get away from me. If I take you back in there, you're going to run away. I know you'll come to love me, though. I just have to distance you from Chad and everyone else for a while," Charlie roared.

He grabbed her arm and started leading her around the pond, farther from the hospital. If he got her too far, she knew her chances of survival became slimmer than they already were. She started fighting against him, but he just pulled harder, laughing like he enjoyed her terror.

***

Chad ran through the parking lot of the hospital grounds, searching for any sign of Bree. He checked each car as it passed him, looking for anything unusual. Nothing! It was like she'd disappeared without a trace.

His phone rang.

"Tell me you have good news," he barked into the mouthpiece.

"Security footage showed she exited the back door about twenty minutes ago," Trenton said with hesitation. Chad tensed.

"A man met her outside; they chatted for a few minutes, then walked toward the trail at the rear of the hospital. The trail leads down to a serenity pond for visitors. Chad, I saw the footage – it was Charlie. I don't know if anything is wrong, but I just… I can't imagine she'd just disappear like that, not with my Dad in here like this…" Trenton trailed off.

Chad changed direction while still holding the phone to his ear.

"How well do you know Charlie?"

"I've known him since high school. I don't… there's no way… I can't imagine him being involved in any of this. Maybe, somehow the stalker found out she was here and ambushed them," Trenton trailed off.

Chad could hear the pain in Trenton's voice. Trenton didn't want to admit it, but it looked like they may have found their perpetrator. His stomach turned as he thought about the man with her. He should have done a better background check on him, but he was Trenton's friend… Chad didn't have time for excuses. He had to get to Bree. Hopefully, she was just sitting at the pond, visiting with an old friend, but his gut told him that wasn't the case.

He found the trail and silently ran down it.

"I'm coming out. We're right behind you," Trenton said before disconnecting the call. He knew Chad was close and wouldn't say anything further.

He shouldn't have let her out of his sight at the hospital. He could've escorted them to the room and waited outside. He had many *what ifs* running through his head, but he knew those didn't do him any good.

Chad felt his adrenaline kick into high gear as he neared the pond. He heard Bree cry out and his body went into fight mode. He had his answer. She was in danger.

He pulled out his gun as he made his way the last several feet. He spotted Charlie dragging Bree down the trail. It looked like he was leading her to the other side. He must have some sort of exit strategy planned. Charlie underestimated Chad.

Chad hid among the trees as he trailed about fifty yards behind them. He tensed when he noticed the gun in Charlie's hand. He'd been afraid of that. Chad couldn't risk Bree getting shot in the heat of battle.

He moved closer as he tried to get a good aim on Charlie. He had no problem shooting the man threatening Bree, but he didn't want Charlie's gun to somehow go off and hurt her. Chad needed to get him to point the gun somewhere else.

"Do you want me to shoot you right here?" Charlie cried when she continued to struggle against him.

"Doesn't that defeat the whole purpose of you wanting us to be together?" she snapped.

"I don't have to kill you, Bree. I can shoot you in the leg, then throw you over my shoulder. The pain is excruciating, but you'll be too busy focusing on that to fight me anymore," he threatened. Chad wanted to beat him to a bloody pulp.

"Just let me go," Bree begged as a tear fell. That seemed to stop him in his tracks.

"I can't, you don't understand. I really do love you."

"This isn't love, Charlie," she sobbed.

"You'll love me, you will," he said with determination.

Chad realized the man had completely lost his mind. Charlie somehow thought he could make her love him. When he realized that wasn't going to happen, he'd have no other choice, at least in his mind, than to kill her. He wouldn't even care if she was pregnant. Heck, as twisted as he was, he'd probably wait until the baby was born, then kill her and take the child, thinking he'd at least always have a piece of her.

Chad would never let the situation get that far. They weren't getting out of his sight. He continued to track them, drawing closer as he waited for his chance to strike.

Charlie grabbed her arm again and pulled her close and Bree threw her head back as she twisted away. She turned in Chad's direction and their eyes locked together. He tried to silently signal her to not give him away, but her eyes softened and her lips turned up in just the barest hint of a relieved smile.

Charlie didn't miss her changed demeanor. He moved faster than Chad expected him to, and whipped their bodies around so Bree was shielding him as he held the gun out and looked into the bushes, straight where Bree had been gazing.

He pressed his finger in and the gun fired, the bullet flying toward Chad. Lucky for him, Charlie was a bad shot. The bullet slammed into the tree two feet to his left, splintering the wood. The man also hadn't been smart enough to place a silencer on the weapon. He'd just given their position away to the rest of Bree's family and probably the entire security force at the hospital.

"It's over, Charlie. Just let her go. Don't make this any worse for yourself," Chad said calmly, keeping his body blocked behind a large tree. He knew the man wouldn't hesitate to put a bullet in him and he'd be no good to Bree if he was dead.

"You got here faster than I thought you would, Chad. If you take one step closer, I'll put a bullet through your bastard child," Charlie snarled.

Chad had no doubt he'd do just that.

"How do you think this can end, Charlie. You know I can't let you take her."

"You don't have a choice," the man screamed as he took a few more steps down the trail, dragging Bree with him. She stared at Chad, her eyes filled with tears.

"Charlie, how do you plan on leaving?"

Chad knew he needed to keep saying his name. The more he humanized him, the more he'd think about the bad choices he was making. He looked to Bree, but only for a moment. He had to keep his eye on Charlie. If he could just get one shot in, that's all it would take to end this whole thing.

Bree started to pull against him and Chad wanted to yell at her not to. He didn't want her getting accidentally shot. He knew Charlie didn't really want to shoot her and only would if he felt he had no other choice.

Charlie ranted at her, then jerked against her chest, causing her head to slam against Charlie's body. He'd pay for the agony he was inflicting on Bree.

"Why, Charlie. Why are you doing this?" Chad asked.

"Do you really need to ask? She's mine and always has been, from the very first time I saw her. She was too young then, so I waited. I watched her date other men, but I knew it wasn't serious. Then, she got on this kick about being independent. I figured that was my perfect time to be with her. She didn't want her family smothering her, but she needed someone. I figured if I scared her a little bit, she'd come running to me. It was perfect, too, because she'd been getting threatening letters. Trenton showed me. It wasn't hard to escalate things to break-in's and stalking. It all would've worked out, too, if you hadn't gotten involved," Charlie sputtered.

"Even if Chad and I hadn't gotten involved, I wouldn't have come to you, Charlie. I wasn't looking for a relationship. I just wanted to focus on me for a while. What happened with Chad and I wasn't planned. It just happened," Bree said gently. She was trying to appeal to the boy she'd known so long.

"You're wrong, Bree. You would've needed me – I know it," Charlie argued. She was telling him they didn't have a chance, yet he was determined to change her mind.

Chad didn't want him to come to the realization that she'd never be his. Once he had nothing to lose, he had no use for her anymore.

"You need help, Charlie. Just let Bree go and we'll get you all the help you need. Trenton's on his way. You don't want him to see you pointing a gun at his sister, do you?"

"He'll understand. He made a comment once, back in high school, that it would be great if Bree and I married, 'cause then we'd be true brothers. I knew then he'd be okay with us being together, no matter how it happened."

If Trenton heard that comment, he'd come unglued. If he had any inkling that he'd played a part in his sister's predicament, he'd be on his knees.

"Why don't we all just sit down and talk about this," Chad offered.

"Get away! I'm not telling you again," Charlie snarled. He pointed his gun toward Chad again and fired, not coming close. Chad was grateful the man had poor aim.

Charlie was moving further down the path and Chad continued to follow. He kept under cover, but didn't let them get more than twenty feet ahead of him. Charlie had to have a car nearby. He'd have to expose himself at that point and that's when Chad would take his shot. There was no way he could let Charlie drive away with her.

"Bree, you'll grow to love me, I promise. I'm a good guy. This day has just gotten kind of messed up. I'll raise your baby, then we'll make more. We could even get rid of this one if you want. Of course that's what you'll want, so we'll have to do that. You may not think so, but you won't want his baby growing inside you. If we just get rid of it, I can plant my seed in you. We'll be a family."

Bree's eyes widened in horror at his words. She started clawing at his arm around her throat. Chad tried to send her a single to calm down, but Charlie was threatening her child and her mother's instincts had kicked in, full-throttle.

"Stop struggling. You're only going to get yourself hurt. If you don't stop now, I'll shoot you, I will, then I'll make sure my shot doesn't miss Chad. He'll rush forward, try to save you, making him such an easy target," Charlie sneered.

His words did their trick. She didn't want to watch Chad get shot, and she knew Charlie was right. If he shot her, Chad would run forward, disregarding his own safety. She couldn't get away from him, so she had to trust Chad wouldn't let her out of his sight. It was the only thing she had to hold on to.

Charlie reached the other side of the pond and started down another trail. She could hear traffic nearby. Bree's heart pounded as she realized they were running out of time. If he managed to get her to his vehicle, Chad wouldn't be able to find them.

"What are you doing, Charlie?" Trenton's voice called out as he rounded a corner, not even trying to take cover.

"Trenton, I know this looks bad, but it's what we've always wanted. Bree's supposed to be mine, and then we'll be related. She just got messed up, being around Chad. It will be fine," Charlie pled with his friend to understand.

"Charlie, let my sister go. We'll sit down and talk. You're hurting her, Charlie," Trenton said as he took a few steps forward.

"You're upset right now, Trenton. Bree doesn't really know what she wants. Chad has her brainwashed," Charlie said.

"Come on, Charlie. We've been friends a long time. You don't want to do this. Let Bree go and we'll talk. We can work this out."

"No! You're brainwashed, too. This man has gotten to all of you. Bree loves me, she does! She wants us to be together," Charlie screamed. The hand that held the gun against Bree's stomach was shaking. He was starting to really lose it and with Trenton distracting him, Chad moved closer. He had to move soon or he might lose Bree.

"This has gone on long enough. Let her go!" Trenton shouted. He stopped talking as a friend and spoke with power in his voice.

Charlie's eyes widened at the tone, and Chad saw the shift in his expression. He was going to make a move.

"You can't talk to me like that," Charlie screamed as he lifted his arm and pointed the gun at Trenton.

"Get down," Chad yelled as he jumped up, his gun aimed at Charlie.

The next few seconds slowed down as several things happened at once. Bree jerked against Charlie's slackened hold and fell to the ground at his feet. Charlie's gun fired, the bullet aiming straight for Trenton. Chad pressed his finger, his deadly aim slamming into Charlie's chest.

Bree blacked out as her head slammed into a rock on the ground. She didn't even have time to know if her brother or Chad were okay.

Chapter Eighteen

Chad ran toward Bree, too late to catch her fall. His insides clenched as he saw blood spread out from her temple. He had to make sure Charlie was down before he could tend to her, though.

He quickly approached the man and kicked his dropped gun out of the way. He knelt by him and placed his fingers on his throat.

Dead.

Charlie wasn't going to hurt anyone else ever again.

"Bree," Trenton called as he stumbled forward.

Chad looked at him, startled by the blood.

"Looks like his aim improved when he was aiming for me," Trenton said, sweat beading on his forehead.

"Where the hell is everyone else?" Chad yelled. Trenton had been shot in the stomach. He needed to be admitted for surgery immediately and Chad still didn't know how bad Bree had hit her head.

He knelt down next to Bree as he heard voices approaching. He gently lifted her head, relieved when he saw only a small cut. Head wounds always bled more than average. He knew it wasn't too bad, but he still wanted her checked into the hospital.

He lifted her in his arms as several people arrived, shouts ringing out around them. Security personnel were there with their guns drawn, and several medical members approaching. One stopped to help Trenton, ordering a stretcher be brought down right away. Another approached Bree.

"I've got her. I'll bring her up to the hospital," Chad insisted. He wasn't letting her out of his arms until he released her into a hospital bed.

"Someone better start talking now," the sheriff yelled as he approached the scene. One person dead on the ground, one passed out, and another bleeding, barely able to keep on his feet.

"This is Bree Anderson's stalker. He was trying to abduct her. I was in pursuit. Her brother showed up, and the situation escalated. The perpetrator, Charlie, aimed and fired at Trenton Anderson, Bree jerked forward, so I had no other choice but to shoot. I don't miss," Chad explained.

There was no need to go into a further explanation at that moment; they'd do that once Bree and Trenton were patched up. He knew all about the paperwork involved when someone was killed, whether it was self-defense, or not.

"Everyone who is not immediately needed, get the hell off my crime scene. Deputy, tape this area off.

The rest of you, get moving. Take the injured into the hospital and anybody who witnessed this, don't even think about leaving. I want statements," the sheriff commanded. Chad had instant respect for the man.

He nodded his assent, then moved quickly up the trail and walked with Bree into the E.R. She got admitted immediately, everyone was already buzzing about the shootout at their serenity pond.

***

Bree woke up in a hospital bed once again and immediately jerked forward. Chad! Trenton! She looked around frantically.

"It's okay, Bree. Everyone is fine," Chad quickly assured her.

"What happened?" she asked, calming when she saw Chad sitting next to her.

Chad quickly filled her in, letting her know Charlie was dead. She lowered her eyes, feeling empathy for the man. She'd known him her entire life and hadn't wanted him dead. He'd needed help, but she couldn't fight the twinge of relief at knowing he wouldn't ever come after her again.

"Trenton is fine. He was shot in the stomach, but it missed all major organs. He came out of surgery a couple hours ago and your family has been going back and forth between your room, your brother's, and your father's. The hospital is filled with Andersons," he finished with a small smile.

"I feel sorry for the staff," Bree said with an attempt at humor.

"Yes, they may go on strike at any moment if Joseph doesn't calm down."

"You're awake," Joseph said as he stepped into the room and nudged Chad out of the way so he could get closer to Bree. "I've been so worried about you. Your father is beside himself."

"I'm fine, Uncle Joseph. Really, I am," Bree assured him.

"You've been through so much. I'm sorry, baby girl."

"I'm not a baby, Uncle," she said, but there wasn't any bite to her words. Joseph leaned down and kissed her on the forehead.

"Chad, I don't know how I could ever express my gratitude to you," Joseph told him.

"You know that's not necessary, Joseph. Your family has always been there for me, and I'm more than happy to do anything at all for you," Chad responded.

"Does that apply to me, too? I have a few things I'd like for you to do for me," Bree said with a wink. She got immense satisfaction at the look of shock on his face.

"I'd go to the ends of the earth for you," Chad replied. Bree couldn't tell if he was serious or not. At times, she just couldn't read him at all.

"Thank you for saving my life. You are everything I'd ever wish for as a father to my child. Strong, passionate, fierce, and the greatest man I know," Bree said. She loved him so very much. She still hadn't had the opportunity to tell him she had her memory back, yet.

"Only because you make me that way," he replied as he bent down and kissed her gently.

"I have something to tell you."

"What is it?" he asked.

"I should've said something sooner, but never had a chance with everything happening so quickly. My amnesia's gone," she finally said.

Bree watched as Chad's eyes rounded. She could see the nervousness in him, but didn't understand why. She would think he'd be happy she had her memories back.

"That's great, baby," he finally said, though he still looked upset.

"I have another confession," she said, her stomach rolling over.

"There's nothing you can say that would upset me," he told her.

"I love you, Chad. I love you so much that the thought of not being with you kills me," she whispered as she looked at him with vulnerability shining in her eyes.

Chad stared at her in wonder for several moments, before his face split in a huge grin. He leaned down and took her mouth with his, kissing her with all of his love and passion. He brought his hand up and caressed her face, loving her so much, he felt close to bursting.

"I'm all for happy moments, but I think I'll leave the two of you alone," Joseph said with a chuckle, then they heard the door quietly close behind him.

"I love you, too, Bree. So much so that the thought of not having you in my life is unbearable. I can't stand the thought of not being with you, not even for one night. You've slowly but surely carved a place in my heart, and now, there's no going back."

All talking ceased as he gently stretched his body out next to hers on the bed and kissed her so intensely, her monitors started going off.

They had to stop when the nursing staff rushed in, thinking something was wrong.

"This is highly inappropriate, Mr. Redington," the nurse scolded while making him climb out of her bed.

"I'm sorry," Bree murmured. The nurse gave her a stern look before leaving the room.

"That was mortifying," Bree admitted.

Chad began laughing before he bent down and gave her one last gentle kiss.

"I'm going to find out how soon I can get you out of here. I want to take you home," Chad said as he rushed from the room to find the doctor.

Bree laid there and wondered how something that had started out so terrifying could end so well. She'd gained her independence only to find she didn't need it. She had a wonderful family she greatly loved and who would always be overprotective, which now didn't seem so bad. She also had a wonderful man who had walked into her life and taken her by complete surprise. Her life had gone from one extreme to the other and that was just fine with her.

It didn't take long for her family to rush through her doors, surround her bed and ask her dozens of questions about her health. She smiled, loving every second of it.

"We've been so worried about you," Jennifer exclaimed as she bent down and gave her a hug.

"You have got to stop getting in shootouts," Amy added with a smile.

"Yes, there are better ways to get a day of pampering other than getting admitted to a hospital," Cassie added.

"I'm thinking a spa would be supremely more comfortable than in here," Jessica joined in with a giggle.

"You know what? I think you're all right. As soon as these people realize I'm fine, you can cart me away for a day of pampering. I think I've earned it," Bree said. She adored her cousins and in-laws. They were wonderful women. She realized the men were starting to get outnumbered at least, with all the marriages and babies being born. She finally didn't feel like the minority.

The men eventually left the women to chat and Bree felt herself relax, enjoying the moments of catching up on all the family gossip.

A little while later, Chad stepped through the door carrying a huge bouquet of mixed flowers and a large bag of chocolate. Ah, a man after her own heart. He stopped in his tracks at the sight of the room full of women. Bree had to fight the giggle wanting to escape at his look of panic.

"I can come back in a while," he said as he set the vase on her nightstand.

"Nonsense, you can be here, too," Jennifer spoke up.

"I'll wait. I want to talk to Bree alone."

"You know she's just going to tell us anything you say, so you might as well talk to her with us here. It saves time," Cassie said with her trademark smile.

Chad looked at each of the women, then at Cassie. He squared his shoulders, then dropped to his knee next to her bed. Bree's eyes widened as she realized what he was doing. The room became instantly silent as all eyes moved from Chad to Bree and back again.

"Brianne Lynn Anderson, I know I asked before, and not in the best way, but circumstances have now changed. I love you with all my heart and I want you by my side each and every day. I want to watch your beautiful body change with the growth of our child, and then I want to do it all over again as many times as you want. I'll treat you like royalty, worship you day and night. I love you and it would be the greatest honor if you'd agree to be my wife," Chad asked. His voice became a bit choked at the end. None of the women in the room could contain their sigh of pleasure at his romantic proposal.

Bree didn't even try to stop the tears cascading down her face. He was everything she could have ever wanted and so much more. She'd never let him get away. From his pocket, Chad retrieved a small box and opened it, showcasing a beautiful solitaire diamond nestled in an exquisite setting.

"Yes, nothing would make me happier," she answered.

Chad gripped her hand, his own slightly shaking as he slipped the ring on her finger. She looked at their joined fingers and knew that's how their life would be.

There was a round of applause and many congratulations as everyone beamed at the happy couple.

"Did I just hear we have a wedding to plan?" Joseph said as he stepped in the room. Bree turned stunned eyes on her uncle. He could be a thousand miles away and hear the word *wedding* if it was spoken by one of his family members.

"Yes, Uncle Joseph, we're getting married," Bree said as she beamed at him, then lifted her hand to show him her beautiful ring.

"Ah, that makes me so happy," he said. "I'm going to go see your father. We have much to do… much to do," he muttered, his head already in planning mode. Bree laughed as he exited the room.

"Do you want to run to Vegas?" Chad asked, only partially kidding. He knew what Joseph was like.

"We could never start our marriage that way. You'll just have to deal with my family," she said, knowing he was man enough for the challenge.

Epilogue

"I knew we could do it, even with your daughter fighting us the entire way," Joseph said as he filled his brother in on Bree's upcoming nuptials.

"I hate being confined to this stinking bed. These doctors are being ridiculous," George pouted.

"I'm with the doctors on this one, brother. You gave us all a good scare," Joseph said with suspiciously bright eyes.

"Don't you start in on that," George choked.

"We've only had our family back together for a couple years. I don't want anything happening now. We have a wedding to plan," Joseph said while taking his brother's hand in his.

"And we still have one child to marry off," George added, the twinkle back in his eye.

"I have a feeling that will be an easy task. Cassie's friend, Kinsey has been here all day, and sparks are still flying between her and Austin. I think the two of them just need a little push. They're running scared, and I think I have the perfect plan in place to give them the shove they both need," Joseph said with delight.

"Don't keep me hanging, Joseph. I need something to do other than watch this terrible television and stare at my monitors," George demanded.

Joseph leaned in and let the planning begin.

See an excerpt from bestselling author, Kathleen Brooks in her break out romance book, Bluegrass State of Mind.

Bluegrass State of Mind

A Bluegrass Series Novel

Kathleen Brooks

Prologue

Her bare feet pounded down the concrete stairs. Her panty hose were ripped from snagging the cold metal strips on the edge of each stair. Her feet stung with every step she took. She heard the door above her open. She pushed herself faster. She couldn't let him catch her.

She jumped the last stair on the sixth floor, the impact of the jump reverberating up her body. She felt as though she had stopped breathing two floors ago. Her lungs burned as she forced her legs to move faster. Her hand was sliding along the railing to brace herself as she raced down the stairs at breakneck speed.

She heard him yell her name. She turned around to see he was now just one floor away. The look cost her dearly as she missed a step and had to slow down to steady herself.

Her heart beat in turn with each slap of her foot. Faster. Louder. She just had to make it to the garage. He would kill her if she didn't. He called her name again as if she were a disobedient child. He was taunting her, triggering her fear. Her heart felt as if it would explode as she ran faster and faster down the stairs.

She didn't feel the cuts causing her feet to bleed. She didn't feel the pain running up her legs. All she knew was she had a couple more flights to go. She tried to suck in a breath of air but could only manage a small gasp. He was closer now. She could feel him right behind her.

The door to the garage was so close. She could see it now. She had to reach it. He closed in on her. She could hear him breathing. She willed her legs to move faster. He reached out his arm to grab her....

Chapter One

McKenna looked around and saw nothing but black, four-plank fences and green grass for as far as she could see. Daffodils were playing peek-a-boo with the bright morning sun. She looked down at the GPS in her cherry red BMW M6. Only five more miles until her destination. Bringing her eyes back up to the narrow country road, Kenna gasped and hit her brakes as hard as she could.

The stabilization in her car kicked in and kept it from fishtailing off the road. She fought for control of the car as her brakes locked. A massive horse was standing in the middle of the road, calmly watching her scrambling for control over her car. She rested her head against the steering wheel and let out a shaky breath when she stopped the car in the opposite lane. Hearing tires squealing, she lifted her head and saw an old pick-up truck heading straight for her, fishtailing out of control. Kenna shifted into reverse and floored it. The truck skidded by her, narrowly missing her car. The truck came to a sudden stop in the grass ditch off the side of the road.

Kenna watched a jeans-clad woman wearing a stylish, black, long-sleeve shirt and bright pink scarf belt jump out of the truck. The woman with beautiful, shiny, shoulder-length brown hair was the polar opposite of what McKenna expected to see. Instead of being concerned about her truck, the woman slowly approached the horse with her hand out. Kenna saw her mouth moving as she talked to him. Ever so slowly, she placed her hand on his head and gave him a smile. Sliding her hand down, she grasped the halter and scratched his nose.

Kenna opened her door and got out on shaky legs. She could hear the woman talking on the cell phone as she walked toward the scene. "Yeah, Bets, I'm out here on Route 178, and it looks like one of your stallions is loose. Another woman and I almost hit him. Yes, we're okay. No, I have him now. You better have one of the boys bring a trailer. Okay. Bye."

"Hi. Are you okay?" Kenna asked after the woman put away the cell phone.

"Yes. Thanks. Looks like you made it out okay. I'm Paige Davies. Do you mind helping me for a sec?"

"McKenna Mason. What do you need?"

"Here, hold this." Paige walked the massive stallion over to her and indicated where she was to hold him. "I need to see if my truck is able to run or if I need to call a tow. Thanks!"

Kenna took a hold of the halter and stared at the horse. She hadn't been around a horse in decades. She held on for dear life, even though the horse seemed content to just stand off to the side of the road and watch the world go by.

Paige's truck roared to life. She drove it out of the ditch and parked next to Kenna's M6. What a sight: a brand new M6 next to a rusted, blue, Chevy pickup that had to be fifteen years old. Paige gracefully jumped down from the cab and walked over to her.

"Thanks. Now we have room for the little guy to be picked up. I wonder how he got out?"

"I'm just glad we didn't hit him."

"This is part of the Ashton Farm, and unfortunately they've been having a lot of problems recently."

"Ashton, as in Will Ashton?" Kenna couldn't believe it. She hadn't even pulled into town and she had just found the person she was looking for.

"Yes. The family owns and runs it. You know Will?"

"I used to. I haven't seen him in seventeen years."

"Are you here to visit them?"

"No, I'm here to interview with Tom Burns for the assistant district attorney job."

"That's great." Paige was so excited for her that Kenna couldn't help but smile. She stepped forward and scratched the forehead of the large horse.

"Actually, I'm glad I ran into someone from the town. Can you tell me a good place to stay? I couldn't find any hotels online."

"That's because there aren't any. You'll want to go see Miss Lily Rae Rose. She has a bed and breakfast. Just continue straight and make a left at the first stop light you come to. She's in the big white Victorian. And, if you're looking for a good place to eat, Miss Lily has two sisters, Miss Daisy Mae Rose and Miss Violet Fae Rose, who run the Blossom Cafe. Great place to eat some chocolate after a close call like this!" Paige laughed and Kenna couldn't help but like her. This was a woman after her own heart!

"Thanks a lot. I'm guessing you're from Keeneston. What do you do there?"

"I have a store on Main Street named Southern Charms. I have all local made products. Everything from statues, paintings, jewelry, clothes, painted wine glasses, to cookbooks."

"Sounds amazing. I'll have to stop by."

"We should have lunch together. I can be the official welcoming party!" They both turned to the sounds of a diesel engine and saw a massive truck with a horse trailer come around the corner from the direction Paige had come. "Ah, good. Now we can get this boy home."

Kenna stood back as three men jumped down from the truck and with an apple helped convince the horse to get in the trailer.

"Thanks for the help with him. I look forward to our lunch. It was great meeting you and welcome to Keeneston," Paige said as she and Kenna walked to their cars.

Kenna's legs had finally stopped shaking when she slid into her car. Pulling out after Paige, she headed into town, wondering what her new home would be like.

*　　*　　*

"Just shoot me now," Kenna thought as she squeezed her eyes closed. She slowly opened them, hoping against all odds the scene before her had changed, but to her utter despair, it was the same scene she had just driven upon. Kenna had pulled her M6 to the side of the road and stared at the town before her with a critical eye. She was sitting on the edge of Main Street and could see the other end of what she guessed to be downtown just two stop lights away. The town was straight out of Mayberry, she thought. She couldn't help but start whistling the theme song to the Andy Griffith Show as she looked around her new hometown: perfect trees lining both sides of Main Street, American flags waving from every light post, and the people wandering down the sidewalk seemed to know each other since they were tipping their hats and smiling to each person they passed by.

Kenna had spent the last eleven years in the Big City. So when she took a deep breath that lacked pollution and listened to the honking of cars that were strangely not honks of anger, but honks of greeting as they passed someone they knew, she felt out of her element. Not for the first time, Kenna wondered how she ended up here. Just a month ago, she was at the hottest nightclub in New York City with her best friend Danielle, celebrating her twenty-ninth birthday with all her friends from Greendale, Thompson and Hitchem, the largest law firm in New York. Kenna sighed wistfully as she thought about the six figure salary, the hot clubs and a condo in the Upper East Side of Manhattan that she had left behind in a hurry.

With her eyes closed and her mind firmly set in what might have been, Kenna thought about how she had dined with professional athletes and actors at the best restaurants on the company dime since they were clients. Standing only five foot four, but blessed with what she called womanly curves, Kenna had not only wined and dined famous people, but had dated and been pursued by some as well. Kenna's auburn hair, milky skin and dark green eyes that hid an intelligence and sharp wit had made her sought after inside and outside of the courtroom.

Kenna continued her trip down memory lane by giving herself a moment to gloat. She had just made junior partner, one of the youngest associates to have ever done so and the only woman to ever do so.

She cringed as she remembered the night it all changed. The night she fled from her six figure salary and left her amazing condo. She had fled from New York City with her ex-boyfriend hot in pursuit of her. Kenna fought a shiver as she remembered Chad trying to find her to prevent her from leaving not only the city but most likely her beautiful condo ever again. It was in the early morning hours of the city that never sleeps that Kenna found herself running for her life and looking for a place to hide. She had sat in her car and thought about what always made her feel better - chocolate. She had suffered a chocolate craving to end all other chocolate cravings that night.

Now sitting in her car in Keeneston, she remembered the shivers of fear that had wracked her body and the feel of the cold bite of the February wind. And all she wanted was chocolate. That's when the idea hit her, the perfect place to hide and the perfect place to indulge in the mother of all chocolate cravings. She had turned her car towards the interstate and headed to Hershey, Pennsylvania.

Kenna's lips twitched. She had been right. Since he had no idea where she was, she was left alone. And in turn, Kenna was surrounded by chocolate for a month. The second night she spent in Hershey, Kenna knew it was time to develop a plan for the rest of her life, or at least for the next phase of her life. Even though she was tempted to apply for the taster's job opening at the Hershey plant, she decided she couldn't waste the law degree her parents' death had paid for. They died when a drunken truck driver jackknifed his semi-truck on a patch of ice, leaving no place for her parents' car to go. The trust they established for Kenna was more than enough to pay for her attendance at law school, and she even had a good part of it left to be able to live off of if she wanted. However, after her parents' death, Kenna had lost the carefree ways that the life of privilege provided and had gone to law school to learn how to put away drunk drivers for the pain they caused innocent families.

Kenna sat on her bed in the extend-a-stay hotel with the smell of chocolate in the air and started looking for a job. She started with Alabama and worked her way through the states alphabetically, looking for places that were hiring. She kept an eye out for cities that were small but not isolated, cities that Chad the Bastard wouldn't think of looking for her. But most importantly, cites that were looking for prosecutors. One week later Kenna pumped her fists in the air and jumped up and down on the bed when she saw the opening for a prosecutor seventeen states later. Not too big, not too small... just right.

It was a good thing she had found the opening when she did, Kenna thought to herself. She couldn't put on any more weight after spending a month in Chocolate Heaven. She pushed the thoughts of the past back in her mind and opened her eyes again. Mayberry was still there. When she was in Hershey the week before, waiting to hear back about an interview, a memory floated up to the surface from some hidden depth of her mind. That memory was Will Ashton. "What the hell," Kenna thought. It's not like she had any place else to go and no idea what the future held besides a job application for an assistant district attorney position. Kenna knew her subconscious had led her here to Will Ashton and to Keeneston, Kentucky.

Kenna pulled herself out of her thoughts as she drove up the driveway, surrounded by Bradford pear trees, and made her way towards the bed and breakfast Paige had recommended. "It's picture perfect," Kenna said to herself as she got out of the car and looked up at the three- story, white brick Victorian.

The green front door opened and a little woman with a helmet of white hair stepped out. "Can I help you, dearie?" she asked Kenna with a soft, Southern tilt to her voice.

"Are you Miss Lily?" Kenna asked as she started up the steps to the wraparound porch.

"Yes, surely I am," Miss Lily answered, her hands clasped in front of her and with a dishtowel casually draped over her shoulder.

"Paige Davies said you had a room to rent for a couple of nights?"

"Yes, I do have a room for you, dearie. Come on in." Miss Lily turned and walked into the house, presuming Kenna would follow right behind.

Kenna turned back to her car, grabbed some of her bags out of the trunk, and hurried into the bed and breakfast just behind Miss Lily. The house was huge with a grand entranceway whose focal point was a wide sweeping staircase. There were large, square shaped rooms off to her right and left.

"Over here are the private quarters," Miss Lily said, pointing to the right. "This first room here on the left is the sitting room for our guests. There are books and such in there, and we have a fire at night in the old fireplace. The room behind the staircase is the dining room."

"I love it."

"Well then, I'll put you on the second floor. If you go up these stairs here, there will be another sitting room. Your room is off to the left."

"Thank you, Miss Lily. I'm McKenna Mason. It's nice to meet you, and thank you for making me feel so welcome in your lovely house."

"Not a problem, dearie. I'll give you a moment to settle in and lunch will be served in an hour," Miss Lily said as she turned to head into what Kenna guessed to be the kitchen.

Kenna grabbed her bags and headed up a staircase obviously made for a different time, a time when ladies wore ball gowns so large they needed the six-foot wide stairs to sweep down while making a grand entrance for a ball.

The sitting room on the second floor was as large as the entrance way and full of overstuffed furniture and a braided rug on the floor. It was the perfect place to curl up and read a book. Two large windows overlooked the front yard and the street. Kenna turned to her left and opened the door to the Man O' War room. She had seen a lot of Man O' War names and couldn't figure why a large and deadly jelly fish was so prominent in Kentucky. Oh well, another Southern mystery she thought as she tugged her bags into the room.

In the center of the room stood a huge, king-sized, four- poster bed so high up, it had little steps to climb up to get into bed. A TV was on top of an old oak dresser that ran the length of the opposite wall. A window seat looked out to the side yard and down towards Main Street. A private bathroom with an iron claw tub finished off the room. It was amazing. Just sitting in the room with the white lace curtains billowing softly with a spring breeze coming in the open window was enough to make her feel safe for the first time since she had left New York City.

Kenna unpacked some of her clothes, put them into the drawers, and went to wash up. It was almost time for lunch and amazing smells were coming up from the kitchen. Her mouth started to water as she thought back to the last meal she had at McDonald's the night before in West Virginia. She finished putting the clothes away and opened the door to head downstairs. The door across the hall from her opened and two impeccably dressed people stepped out. They were dressed casually, well, as casually as you can be dressed in Ralph Lauren, Kenna noted.

"Oh, we have another guest!" sang the women. She was a couple inches taller than Kenna and in her early forties. Her makeup was perfect in that understated way only movie stars could manage. Her blond hair was pulled into a perfect pony tail tied off with a white ribbon. Kenna realized that if one wasn't used to shopping the expensive department stores like she was, one would never know the woman was wealthy, well, except for the eight carat diamond weighing down her ring finger. Compared to this bubbly woman, Kenna felt much older than her twenty-nine years after the pressure and stress of the last month. Kenna pasted on a smile and turned to face the perky couple.

"So we do, honey," her husband said to her. He matched her perfectly. Kenna placed him at fifty years old and dressed in Ralph Lauren jeans and a white button up shirt. His salt and pepper hair was perfectly trimmed. He let his right hand rest lightly at the small of his wife's back.

"Are you here for the sales as well?" Mrs. Perky Ralph Lauren asked Kenna.

"Sales? I didn't see any department stores in Keeneston. I could do a little shopping." A happy feeling washed over her and Kenna's smile turned into a real one. The kind of feeling that only spending money on the perfect pair of sexy shoes or finding that little black dress that hid ten pounds and increased your bust at least one cup size could do for you.

"Oh! Oh, ha, a joke. Good one, little lady."
Mr. Ralph Lauren laughed. Kenna darted a glance
back and forth between the couple, and apparently
Mrs. Perky picked up on her creased brow and look
of utter confusion at the apparent joke she had made.

"Julius, she's not joking. Dear, I'm so sorry.
We thought any visitors would be here for the
Keeneland horse sales."

So, Mr. Ralph Lauren was Julius. Apparently
they had come from out of town, out of state by
Kenna's guess, for horse sales. That was good news
for her since she had found out Will still has a horse
farm.

"I am so sorry. Since June and I are so horse
crazy, I just assumed you were too. I'm Julius Kranski
and this is my wife, June." Julius turned and took his
hand off his wife's back to shake Kenna's.

June clasped Kenna's hand and lightly held
onto it when she introduced herself to Kenna. "So
nice to meet you!"

"Nice to meet you both. I'm McKenna Mason,
but you can just call me Kenna. It's nice to meet some
other people from out of town. Where are you from?"
she asked as she looked back at June.

"We have a horse farm in Ocala, Florida,"
June said as she smiled and gently squeezed Kenna's
hand again.

She's a toucher, Kenna thought as June continued, "I hope we can be friends. I always love coming to Miss Lily's for the sales. We always meet the most wonderful people." June continued to talk as Kenna made her way to the dining room for lunch, explaining all about the sales and about the horses they were hoping to buy. Kenna looked around the dining room and noted that it was casually set with a buffet of olive nut and pimento cheese sandwiches. Fresh fruit was in a bowl and a large salad was set in the middle of the round table were Kenna sat with June and Julius.

"Come in, come in. Have a seat just anywhere at the table ya'll. I'll be out in a jiffy with the sweet tea," Miss Lily said as she quickly zipped into the kitchen. Kenna's eyes widened slightly. Miss Lily was remarkably fast for someone in her early seventies. She reappeared with a pitcher of sweet tea, and her white apron was blown back from her flowered dress as her easy spirits sailed across the polished hardwood floors. The room was bright with sun streaming in through the open windows.

Kenna picked up her sweet tea, tentatively gave it a sip, and found that she was pleasantly surprised by the taste. Julius and June began to talk about one of the horses they were hoping to sell and which barns they should go to first when they went to the Keeneland sales after lunch as Kenna listened with half an ear and nibbled at the pimento cheese sandwich. Not bad, she thought and then took a bigger bite.

"So, are these horse sales a big deal? I mean, do lots of people go to them?" Kenna asked while she tried the olive nut sandwich. She was definitely going to have to learn how to make these sandwiches and had a feeling Miss Lily would teach her in a heartbeat if she asked.

"They sure are, hon," Julius told her. "The Keeneland sales bring in tens of millions of dollars every year. There are smaller sales in Florida and some good sized sales in Saratoga, New York. But if you want the next big thing or the best selection, you go to Keeneland."

"It's also the best place to see the who's who of racing," June chimed in. "For example, some Middle Eastern royalty own racing stables. There's a Sheik from some small oil country who's trying to build the next big stable right here in Keeneston. He's not the only royalty. Queen Elizabeth has been known to have a horse or two stabled in the area. She's also attended the Derby a couple of years ago."

Kenna though that this was as good a time as any to ask about one of the reasons she had come to Keeneston , "When I was a kid, one of my Nana's friend's family had a horse farm here. This morning I found out the Ashtons are still here. Do you know them?"

"The Ashtons!" June practically squealed. She clapped her hands lightly together and beamed at Kenna, "Of course we know them. Everyone knows them. After all, they have Spires Landing at stud on their farm here in Keeneston."

Kenna breathed a sigh of relief and felt a little of the weight lift off her shoulders. Maybe June would know how to get in touch with Will. That would be easier than trying to find the entrance to the farm. She would feel strange just knocking on the door. "So, you think they'll be at the sales?"

"Of course, although I don't know if Betsy and William will be there. But I'm sure someone from the family will be," June said.

Will had gotten married. Kenna knew it was wishful thinking or stupidity on her part to think that after all these years he wouldn't be married. After all, he was a couple years older than she, probably around thirty-two by now. She had heard that he had graduated from the University of Kentucky and played in the NFL for a couple of years, so it was definitely stupid to think him still unmarried. Childhood crush aside, she needed help and he was the one she was depending on to give it to her.

"If you want to go to the sales this afternoon, we'd be happy to take you. Wouldn't we, sugar?" June said, interrupting Kenna's thoughts.

"Of course we would. You just come along with us if you'd like," Julius responded.

Kenna looked at her phone calendar and saw that her appointment with the Keeneston District Attorney's office was scheduled for two days from now, so time was a concern. It was best to go track down Will now and beg him to put in a good word with her potential boss. Or see if he knew of any other jobs in town if she didn't get the D.A. job. "That would be great. Thanks, June, Julius."

After finishing lunch, Kenna went to freshen up before heading out to the sales. She stared at her hair in the mirror and attempted to fluff it, but then it just ended up looking tangled as opposed to that Hollywood, windswept 'just had great sex' look. She looked at her clothes hanging in the closet and decided to compensate for not having the 'just had great sex' hair with her own Ralph Lauren skin- tight, green cable sweater. Mr. and Mrs. Perky put her in the Ralph Lauren mood. She slipped her small feet into her black Nine West, two- inch heel boots to boost her shortened height up to what she thought of as a normal height. With that, she was ready to go. Wiping sweaty hands on her jeans, she headed downstairs, trying to prepare herself for what would equate to begging and pleading for help finding a job, something she never, never, never did, especially from an old crush she thought as she rolled her eyes, who would probably not even remember her name.

Kenna found the Kranskis on the wraparound porch and walked with them down the stone path lined with daffodils. She slid into the back seat of their white Mercedes sedan.

She looked out the window as they headed toward the "big city" of Lexington. She guessed being from New York City, anything under a couple million people seemed small, but she could understand if you're from the surrounding towns of fewer than twenty-five thousand people, that Lexington with its population of three hundred thousand would be a "big city". As she stared out the window, she felt some comfort come over her as she watched the rolling hills of the farmland dotted with corn, tobacco, soy bean, cows, horses and beautiful manor houses pass by. So open and so green… she had never seen so much green.

Fifteen minutes later they approached Keeneland and turned with a steady stream of traffic into the race track. Kenna observed the beautiful landscaping and how open it seemed while at the same time a huge plane was attempting a landing over the racetrack.

"The airport is right across the street," Julius explained. "That was probably one of the Sheiks or a Royal from somewhere across the pond coming in for the sales. They'll fly into the small airport and just park the plane for a day or two."

She nodded, showing she had been listening to him. Kenna thought it was safe to bet the owner of that plane was going to inject some cash into the thoroughbred industry.

They drove through fields of green grass, all trimmed and lined with huge old trees, up to a clubhouse. A valet came out and took the keys from Julius and went to park the Mercedes. Julius and June started a constant stream of chatter between themselves and then deftly went through the clubhouse to the paddock area. Pictures of past Derby winners and stakes winners lined the stone walls from the times they had raced at Keeneland. The majesty of the pictures, the feel of the stone building, the sounds of the horses' hooves, and smelling the scents of cut grass, hay, oats and leather, she could just feel the history of the place and start to understand why horse racing has been such a popular sport for hundreds of years.

They stepped out of a stone walkway and into the paddock where horses were being led around with a number stuck to their hips. Hundreds of people were milling about, looking at each horse or just talking to one another. Some people where wearing Armani suits
while some were in worn cowboy boots and faded jeans. She caught the sight of one man in a simple button- up shirt, faded jeans with some tears in it, and boots that looked like they had stepped in nothing but horse crap. Yet he pulled out a state of the art Smartphone and had the keys for an Audi carelessly dangling out of his pocket. She smiled at the strange scene. Who these people were, what they wore, and the type of car they drove was of no importance. Audi driving cowboys chatted with beat- up Ford truck owners over which horse to bid on.

Taking in another deep breath, Kenna closed her eyes and let the sounds and scents flow over her. Having always been a history buff, she could just see the men and women walking around in 1936 when Keeneland first opened. While she had been daydreaming, the Kranskis had made their way across the paddock and were heading for a string of barns.

"We're heading over to the Spring Creek Barn to check out a yearling. You see that blue and white flag over the third barn down? That's the Ashton Barn. Just make your way down there and ask for your friend. Whenever you're done, just come find us." And with that, June gave Kenna a finger wave and started to walk toward another barn. Find them? How, could she find them in this massive place?

She took a deep breath and turned toward the blue and white flag. As she walked towards it, she passed by a couple of barns proudly displaying certain colors she took to be the farm colors, much like a family crest. She slowed as she approached the Ashton Barn and saw that many people walking horses around were all wearing blue and white polo shirts. It must be a way to identify farm personnel. Some were taking horses up to the paddock while others were putting them in stalls. Still others took them out of stalls and walked them to groups of people who seemed to be examining them. Kenna assumed that they were potential buyers. She looked around and didn't see anyone she guessed to be Will. Of course, the last time she had seen him she was twelve and he wasn't quite sixteen. However, she didn't think she would ever forget those dark, chocolate brown eyes. She looked around, scanning the faces around the barn.

She sighed as she realized she needed help finding him and turned to the closest man in the blue and white uniform, "Excuse me, I'm looking for Mr. Ashton. Is he here today?" she asked the short young man leading a horse from the barn.

"Si. He over there," the blue and white clad man said in broken but understandable English. He pointed to a little hallway in the middle of the barn. It was lined with more horse stalls, and as she approached, she saw a man rubbing the nose of one of the horses. He was tall, at least six feet one inch, and his brown hair had a slight amount of gray in it near his temple. He still looked good though, even if he was a little prematurely gray.

She walked up behind him and stood for a moment staring at his back, trying to figure out how to say, "Hi, I know you haven't seen me in seventeen years, but I was hoping you could help me start a new life here in Kentucky by helping me get a job and maybe find a place to live."

Before she could make her presence known, Will turned to her and asked, "You here to look at Miss Thing, hon?"

Kenna's mouth opened, but nothing came out. She stood momentarily locked in place taking him in. The graying hair, the brown twinkling eyes, the huge smile that showed one dimple on his left cheek, the wrinkles around his eyes, and the hands gave away his

age. It wasn't Will. She let out the breath she hadn't realized she was holding, "I'm sorry. I was told Mr. Ashton was in here," Kenna said with a distracted smile on her face. She was fighting off the strange feeling that she knew this man, but couldn't place him.

"Well, then you found him. William Ashton. Nice to meet you, ma'am." Mr. Ashton stepped forward with his hand outstretched. Kenna stared for a second and then reached her hand out to grasp his. He gently, yet firmly shook her hand and gave her an approving nod when she returned the firm handshake.

See an Excerpt from The Tycoon's Revenge by Melody Anne
Chapter One

Derek Titan looked around the crowded room and had to force himself not to yawn. He couldn't stand attending events where everyone drank too much, laughed too loud and tried far too hard to impress each other.

Derek knew he was what women considered a real catch. Hell, a stupid magazine had done a write up on Seattle's most eligible bachelors and placed his picture as number one. He'd been furious and tried to have himself taken out of the article but his attorney had spouted some crap about freedom of speech. Since the article, he was being approached by even more materialistic females.

The magazine listed his net worth as equal to Bill Gates. They'd also said he was tall, dark and handsome. He stood over six feet, with broad shoulders and muscles that rippled throughout his entire body. He hated gyms but he ran every morning and sometimes in the evenings too. He'd discovered at a young age running was a great form of relieving his stress.

He knew the second best way to relieve stress was to take a woman to bed. The minute he was done with her, he walked away, though. There were many women who tried to get him to stay but no one held his interest longer than it took him to button up his pants.

After his heart had been shattered by Jasmine, he wasn't interested in any other woman. He figured once he got his revenge, he'd think about settling down.

A woman breezed by him wearing entirely too much perfume and he snapped back to reality. He sighed as he grabbed a glass of wine from a passing waiter.

These parties were all about who had the most to offer. The women were on the prowl and the men were fishing. He wasn't interested. If he wanted a woman, he could have one at any time. He wasn't interested in superficial, wanna-be socialites.

He watched as a couple of ladies passed by, dripping in diamonds and low cut gowns. They were trying to catch his eye and normally he'd make their day by flirting a little, giving them the impression they stood a chance but today wasn't that day. He had a raging headache and he was pissed he'd been summoned.

"There you are, boy. What are you doing hiding in the corner?" Daniel Titan, his father, walked up and questioned him.

"I'm wondering why I'm here when I'd rather be home with a scotch and my feet up," Derek replied.

"You're here because you received a request from your father. I have some things to discuss with you later," Daniel said in his no nonsense voice.

"And it couldn't wait until later?" Derek questioned.

"Oh live it up a little. You're always so busy adding a few more million to your bank account you don't stop to smell the roses," his father admonished him.

"I live it up plenty, hell I was in Milan last week."

"You were in Milan on business, that doesn't count," his dad told him, a bit exasperated.

"For me, the ideal time is mixing business with pleasure," Derek told his father, with a waggle of his brows. Both men relaxed.

"Seriously, Dad I do have a headache. What's so important it couldn't wait until morning?" Derek asked. Once Derek had made his first million he'd moved his father to the city and Daniel was the Chief Financial Officer of his huge corporation. His father was brilliant and had helped the company grow further. His dad may have had several hard times while Derek was growing up but he was essential to Derek's company now.

"David Freeman's here tonight and he's talking to some people, trying to get investors," Daniel answered him. Derek was on instant alert. He searched the room, spotting his enemy. He was the one who'd made him the cut throat business man he'd turned into.

"It's far too late for him. By tomorrow morning his company will be mine, no matter what he tries tonight," Derek said with a sneer.

As Derek watched David, a beautiful woman approached him, stepping up on her tip toes to kiss him on the cheek. David didn't even bother to turn and acknowledge her, which she didn't seem to notice. The man noticed nothing around him if it didn't have dollar signs on it, not even his stunning daughter. Derek's eyes narrowed to slits. He hadn't seen Jasmine for ten years and those years had been very good to her.

Her dress was skin tight on top, dipping low in both the front and back. Her curves were even more pronounced now that her body had matured. She had dark hair, which was swept up in a classic bun, with tendrils floating around her delicate face. Her dark brown eyes had once mesmerized him. They had a hypnotic quality, with their deceiving innocence shining through and the thick, dark lashes surrounding them.

He was angry at the tightening in his gut at just the sight of her. She'd nearly destroyed him and yet he still wanted her. His full revenge included her though, so he'd have her in his bed again and then she'd be begging him not to leave.

"I'm leaving now. He won't make any progress tonight and tomorrow's a busy day for me. I appreciate you calling, though," Derek said. He then turned away and walked out of the room, without once looking behind him.

Jasmine spotted Derek across the room and her insides went up in flames. She narrowed her eyes in anger at the man as he walked around like he owned the place. She knew the kinder, gentler side of him but that boy was long gone. He may have never really existed beyond her imagination.

He wasn't the boy who had taken her virginity and promised her forever. She thought back to that summer so many years ago. She'd waited at the abandoned church all day hoping something had happened to make him run late. When the sun had faded from the sky she'd finally had to admit he wasn't coming. It had all been lies.

She watched him now, as he turned and walked from the room. He was by far the sexiest man in the room, with his custom tuxedo and piercing blue eyes. He had a delectable body, even though he sat in an office all day. Her heart fluttered, remembering those long summer nights of running her hands and tongue down those hard muscles.

She had no idea her world was about to flip upside down. She was soon to learn the man she thought of as her hero, her father, wasn't who she really thought he was. This would truly be her last night of innocence. When morning came, nothing would ever be the same again.

As Derek disappeared around the corner, she couldn't help but think back to the summer ten years before. It had been a time when she'd really believed in fairytales and magic.

She'd grown up very wealthy in the small town outside of Seattle Washington. Her father owned a multi-million dollar company and she'd always had more than most people could ever hope for.

He'd chosen their home in the small town, she'd thought so she could live in a nicer area. She'd later learn he'd really chosen to live there so he could be the big man on campus. He liked lording his wealth over all those around him but she didn't know any of that then. She'd been young and naïve. She'd learn in the next few months how much her father had kept from her.

Her mother died during childbirth so she'd never known her. Her father never remarried, though he dated a lot of women. None of them really acknowledged her presence so she didn't get attached to any of them. Sometimes, she thought it would be nice to have a woman help her pick out a dress or teach her how to do her hair. The staff was great and always spoiled her a bit, which irritated her father.

She'd seen Derek in school from the time she was young but she really got to know him the summer before her senior year in high school. He'd been from the proverbial wrong side of the tracks. His family was dirt poor but he was always determined to make a success out of his own life and turn things around. He ended up helping her with her math and soon they were inseparable. She'd loved his hunger and motivation and the way he never talked down about anyone. She thought he was every one of her fairytales come to life.

She found she was spending every waking moment with him. When her father found out she was dating a boy from the poor side of town he'd been furious and demanded her to end the relationship. It was the first time in her life her father told her she couldn't have something she wanted. It also was the first time she'd defied him.

She'd been stubborn, putting her foot down and continued to see Derek behind her father's back. She loved that he seemed to like her for her and not her money. He wouldn't let her spend money on him, ever. He worked hard for a construction company, which would frustrate her at times, because she wanted him to be with her and not at a job.

He'd just laugh but always made it up to her on the weekend. That last weekend they'd been together they snuck off and went camping in the woods. She'd made love to him for the first time. It was the most magical experience she'd ever had. He proposed marriage to her that night and she said yes. They were going to meet at the old abandoned church on the outside of town on Sunday and run away together. He'd been saving all his money and was heading to the city to make something of himself.

She'd gone home, after being gone all night and her father had been spitting he was so angry with her. She'd told him she was of legal age and could do what she wanted. She told her father she loved Derek and she was going to marry him. Her father had seemed to accept her decision, because he'd become eerily calm and kissed her on the cheek. That was a rare thing as he wasn't normally a man to openly show affection.

He said she was right and he was proud of her for making adult decisions. He then asked if he could help with anything. She'd been so happy her dad accepted her decision she told him everything.

The next day she ended up being late to the church, because she had a few errands her dad had asked her to do for him. She knew she had the rest of her life with Derek so she could wait a couple of hours to run away with him. She knew he'd wait for her. She was confident in their relationship.

She got to the church and was surprised he wasn't there but figured he'd gotten busy like her. She waited and then waited some more. She sat there all afternoon until she finally accepted he wasn't coming as the sun started to set in the sky.

She'd dragged herself home, crying the entire way. When she walked into the house and her father saw her, he'd taken her into his arms and asked her what was wrong. She'd cried against him and finally told him Derek hadn't shown up.

He continued to stroke her back and tell her everything was okay. He'd explained to her he never trusted the boy and that's why he'd been so overprotective. She never suspected her father had anything to do with Derek not arriving.

Derek left the hotel and was thinking back to that summer as well but his memories were far different from those of Jasmine's. He had so much bitterness about that day but if he really thought back to it that's what shaped him into the man he was now.

He'd fallen head over heels for the girl. He'd never thought he was worthy of dating someone as amazing as her but he was determined to make himself so. When he ended up helping her with her school work and found a connection together, he was unable to stay away from her.

He thought she was so different from the other kids who had money. Her family was the richest in town and her father reveled in that fact. He walked around in his custom made suits and drove his expensive cars. Hell, the man's house was a showpiece so all the people lower than him could worship at his doorstep.

When he and Jasmine made love for the first time and he'd realized she'd given him her most sacred gift, he was overwhelmed. He proposed right away and decided to run away with her, to do the right thing.

He planned on heading to the city and making something of himself so he could continue to give her all the things she was used to. He wanted to make sure she never went without anything. He wanted to place her on a throne and spoil her rotten. He'd do or give her anything she wanted.

He'd shown up at the church full of naïve teenager dreams and one bag. When he heard approaching steps, he'd turned in anticipation. His heart sunk at the sight of her father. The man approached with a sympathetic smile plastered on his face.

"Derek, I'm sorry but Jasmine asked me to come and speak with you," David had stated. Derek didn't understand why she'd send her father. "Jasmine said she couldn't face you but she didn't want to leave here. I have some cash here to help you on your way. She said you planned to go to the city and I want to help you get there," he said with that same smile on his face.

Derek felt like his world was falling out underneath him. The man pulled out an envelope loaded with hundred dollar bills. He held it out towards Derek. David was trying to pay him off. It was as if he was saying, *thanks for entertaining my daughter but your services are no longer needed.*

"I don't want your money," Derek spat at him. David continued holding the envelope out, like he couldn't believe the kid from the wrong side of town wouldn't jump at having that much cash.

"Jasmine was hoping this would appease your feelings and help you get on with your life," David had the gall to say.

"Tell Jasmine no thank you," Derek growled at him and then turned and walked away. He never looked back. He'd been pissed when David had offered to pay him off but when he found out it was Jasmine's idea he saw red.

He couldn't believe how wrong he'd been about her. The thing that made him even angrier was the grief coursing through him at knowing he wouldn't see her again. As he walked back towards his childhood home he vowed someday he'd have her begging him to take her back and then he'd be the one to walk away.

He'd made his way home, told his father goodbye and then left for the city. He worked night and day until he purchased his first company. He was excellent at his job. He found companies that were on the verge of bankruptcy, bought them and divided them up, making huge sums of money. His first takeover had led to many, many more. He was now worth far more than Jasmine ever had been and he was about to exact his revenge.

He downed a scotch and then went to bed. His day would be a full one tomorrow and he wanted to be well rested for what was to come. He'd finally have Jasmine at his mercy, when her daddy no longer had any money left.

Runaway Heiress

ABOUT THE AUTHOR

Melody has had a passion for writing since she was a young girl. Her first book was written around the age of ten, about a handsome Prince Charming rescuing his princess and taking her away to his castle to live happily ever after. She continued to write through her teenage years, but never with the expectation to publish. Around 2007 Melody realized she had finished her first full manuscript, and looked at it in awe. She had around a hundred books started on her computer, but had never finished one. She was so ecstatic about her accomplishment that she jumped in to work on another book. She finished five books in a three year period, and then started thinking about possibly publishing those books.

Once Melody published, she has been in author's bliss. She is thrilled by the success of her books, since she loves her characters, and wants the world to feel the same way. She is always working on new material, and feels like the sky is the limit. Her family helps come up with many ideas, and her friends are a constant help.

Melody has two amazing children, along with about five additional kids that she adores like her own kids, who keep her busy all the time with school events, and sporting schedules. She has a wonderful husband who has become a great cook since she is in front of her computer all the time, and two puppies, who help her writing by making sure to keep her lap or feet warm. Family is always first in her life.

Made in the USA
Lexington, KY
21 January 2013